Dear Reader,

Fairy tales gave me my first addictive taste of fiction—addressing subjects which were often forbidden to a child. Power. Jealousy. Ambition.

And the lengths to which people would go to achieve their heart's desire...

Good fought evil in worlds very different from mine. Magical worlds—transformed by a word or the wave of a wand. Houses were made of gingerbread, and pumpkins became glittering carriages—while a frog was really a handsome prince!

It's that transformative quality which underpins my grown-up fairy tale about Corso and Rosie, based on "Snow-White and Rose-Red" (spoiler: no dwarfs or wicked stepmothers!). Instead, two royal brothers—one with a childhood curse—pit their wits against two beautiful sisters.

The first story features Corso, who has ruthlessly eradicated all emotion, because a king cannot afford to be vulnerable. Can ordinary Rosie Forrester melt the ice surrounding his heart?

Yes...but only by magic. The most powerful magic of all.

You know what I mean. It's around us all the time, but sometimes we don't open our eyes wide enough to see it.

It's called *love*.

Look out for Bianca's story—coming soon...

Sharon xx

Sharon Kendrick once won a national writing competition by describing her ideal date: being flown to an exotic island by a gorgeous and powerful man. Little did she realize that she'd just wandered into her dream job! Today she writes for Harlequin, and her books feature often stubborn but always to-die-for heroes and the women who bring them to their knees. She believes that the best books are those you never want to end. Just like life...

Books by Sharon Kendrick

Harlequin Presents

Cinderella in the Sicilian's World
The Sheikh's Royal Announcement
Cinderella's Christmas Secret
One Night Before the Royal Wedding
Secrets of Cinderella's Awakening
Confessions of His Christmas Housekeeper

Conveniently Wed!

His Contract Christmas Bride

Jet-Set Billionaires

Penniless and Pregnant in Paradise

Visit the Author Profile page
at Harlequin.com for more titles.

Sharon Kendrick

STOLEN NIGHTS
WITH THE KING

PRESENTS

ISBN-13: 978-1-335-58355-0

Stolen Nights with the King

Harlequin Enterprises ULC
22 Adelaide St. West, 41st Floor
Toronto, Ontario M5H 4E3, Canada
www.Harlequin.com

Printed in U.S.A.

This book is dedicated to the amazing anthropologist Winifred Creamer, whom I was lucky enough to meet on a long-distance train journey in Australia (Darwin to Adelaide, if you're interested!).

Her skill was in explaining the past and making it come alive with breathtaking clarity. It's what helped make this story extra special.

STOLEN NIGHTS
WITH THE KING

CHAPTER ONE

AGAINST THE GLARE of the beach, the man seemed to blaze more brightly than the sun. His tall body was bronzed. The sunlight caught his thick hair and gilded it with licks of fire, making him appear almost incandescent. But unlike everyone else on the beach, Rosie wasn't particularly mesmerised by his presence. She wasn't trying to get him to notice her, or stare at her. Mostly she was trying to melt into the background and pretend she wasn't there, wishing she were back home in England.

She glanced across the sand, where everyone looked like models you might see within the pages of a glossy magazine. She'd always been taught to concentrate on the similarities rather than the differences between people, but here there *were* no similarities and never had she felt it more keenly than today. She was different from everyone else who frolicked on the fine-grained silver sand.

She wasn't royal.

She wasn't even well connected.

And she certainly wasn't rich.

Fiddling with the strap of her black swimsuit, she continued to observe the action playing out on Monterosso's most desirable stretch of beach, where the assembled gathering was paying homage to the man in their midst. The man with a mane of hair which some called russet, or titian, but was often described in gushing newspaper profiles as resembling dark fire. He exuded an aura of poise and power. Of arrogance and assurance. Every woman was in love with him and every man strove to be like him.

Corso.

Or, more accurately, Corso Andrea da Vignola, Prince and heir to the fabulous kingdom of Monterosso, with its casinos and nightclubs and the famous red mountain which had given the country its name.

Women wearing bikinis, which looked as if they had been constructed from dental floss, opened their glossy mouths and roared with laughter whenever the Prince spoke. They thrust out their perfect breasts and sucked in already concave stomachs as they unsubtly vied to capture his interest. They looked like thronging cattle in a market stall, Rosie thought in disgust, quickly quashing the thought that she might perhaps be *jealous* of them. Of course she wasn't. For a period in her life she'd felt almost close to him, before time and circumstances had intervened. These days she felt as if she didn't know him, apart from the fearsome reputation he seemed to have acquired in the press—*the playboy with the heart of stone*, they called him, although Rosie thought that was a bit cruel. Just because a man of twenty-five hadn't chalked up much in the way of long-term relationships, didn't necessarily mean he had a heart of stone, did it?

Her bottom pressing into the sand—for all the loungers had been taken and she was too shy to ask for another—she folded her arms around her knees, hoping the pose struck a confidence she was far from feeling. She wondered how much longer she was going to have to stay here with her head getting hotter and hotter beneath her cheap sunhat. Probably until Corso decided he wanted to leave—because it was forbidden for a guest to leave a function before the royal Prince.

Why *had* she come here?

She should have let the past go. Let it slip

away like a silent stream, into the hidden back-waters of her mind.

She stared down at the grains of sand, which looked like crushed diamonds as they glittered in the sunshine. Had she been hoping to find a sense of peace, of belonging—here in this Mediterranean paradise where she had spent so many happy summers, before life had hurled a series of grenades into her life? Perhaps she had. But, like all daydreams, her hopes had dissolved the minute they'd made contact with reality. She had no place here, not really. Her imaginings had been nothing but illusions. Although her father had been considered Monterosso's most respected archaeologist and the Prince's favoured mentor, when it boiled down to it, he had been nothing more than a servant.

And she, a servant's daughter.

'Now, the question I am asking myself is what you're doing over here, hiding away in the shadows like a lynx in the forest. Why aren't you joining in with the party?'

Rosie was startled by the sound of a richly accented drawl, which had always been the most distinctive voice she'd ever heard. She glanced up to see Corso standing in front of her and quickly turned to look behind her to see who he was talking to, but there was no-body there.

'Yes, I'm speaking to you, Rosie.'

His deep voice was tinged with amusement but it sounded as if it might be underpinned with a faint sense of impatience and Rosie realised that she must have looked the odd one out among all the supermodels, world-class sportswomen and other over-achieving females who were on the beach-party list. She should have listened to her sister, who had told her she would be insane to pitch up at one of the most glittering social events of the year, taking her hopelessly inadequate wardrobe with her. But Rosie had felt drawn back to Monterosso, as if she were being tugged there by an insistent and invisible string. Was that because some of her happiest times had been here, in this beautiful mountain kingdom—or because the current reality of her life was grey enough to make her want to lose herself in the past?

And, of course, Bianca had been right, because everything *did* seem strange and different—which was probably more to do with the way Rosie was feeling, rather than the way she looked. Had she imagined that she might have some sort of special bond with the Prince, just because he used to enjoy her mother's chicken pie and had taught her how to tie knots? Because if she had, then surely *that* was the real insanity.

Once she might have chattered to him with the lack of inhibition of a child, but now she didn't dare. She couldn't think of a single thing to say. She shifted awkwardly, self-conscious of her under-developed body and how gauche she must seem compared to all the stunners who were draped across the sand. Which was why she stayed exactly where she was, unwilling to stand up and subject herself to the scrutiny of the royal Prince, who suddenly seemed like a stranger to her. How could it be that the man she had once regarded as a quasi-big brother— if their positions in life hadn't been so dramatically different—now appeared so distant and remote? She could feel her cheeks growing hotter and she swallowed. If this was what growing up was about then she didn't want it.

'Happy birthday, Corso,' she said awkwardly.

'Thank you,' he responded, with a regal inclination of his head.

But his dark brows remained raised in question and Rosie realised to her horror that he might be expecting her to bow down before him. Was he? As a child, she had only ever curtseyed to his father, the King, and the Corso she had known would have loathed such for-

mality. Cheeks still burning, she scrambled to
her feet, painfully aware of the plain swimsuit
which emphasised her bony ribs and skinny
legs. As she sank towards the soft sand, she
wished it would swallow her up.

'Forgive me for my lack of protocol,' she said
as she rose to her feet once more. 'I'm not quite
sure what to do. Not any more.' He was looking at her in bemusement—as if he was unused
to someone saying exactly what was on their
mind—and something about the molten quality of his golden gaze made her blurt out the
truth. 'It's so weird being back here.'

'Yes, I can imagine it must be.' There was a
pause. 'How long has it been?'

'Six years.'

'Six years? Is it really?'

Was that a sigh she heard? Surely not. Sigh-
ing was something she associated with senti-
ment or nostalgia—and the steely Corso was
not the type of man to indulge in either.

'Time passes with the speed of a tornado,'
he continued, with a frown. 'How old are you
now? Sixteen?'

Rosie shook her head. She knew she was
young-looking for her age, but for some stupid reason his comment hurt. Surely she hadn't
expected him to remember how old she was!

'Eighteen,' she amended. Which made him twenty-five. But Corso looked like a fully grown man, in the first great flush of his vibrant prime, whereas she felt gawky and naïve in comparison.

His handsome face grew grave. 'I miss your father,' he said suddenly.

Rosie nodded, her heart giving a sudden wrench. 'We all miss him,' she said, and the thought of the man she had idolised made her remember her manners. 'It was very…very kind of you to invite me here, to your birthday celebrations.'

'I thought it might please you all to revisit a place he loved so much.' His eyes narrowed into a metallic gleam, which was suddenly tinged with hardness. 'Although I was surprised your mother and sister were unable to accompany you.'

Rosie bit her lip. It was a statement which managed to be a question and a rebuke all at the same time because clearly the Crown Prince of Monterosso wasn't used to people turning down one of his coveted invitations. 'Er, no,' she said. 'I'm afraid they couldn't make it.'

There was little point in enlightening him that her mother had gone to pieces ever since her husband had died, or that Bianca had sworn never to set foot on Monterosso again. She remembered what her sister had said when Corso's gilt-edged invitation had unexpectedly thudded onto the mat.

'Who wants to be reminded of a place where we had to be grateful for every damned thing we got?' Bianca had demanded. 'Which robbed us of everything that mattered to us?'

Deep down, Rosie disagreed with Bianca's anti-Monterossian views, but she didn't attempt to talk her out of them, because her older sister was far too strong-minded. And besides, Bianca was at university now. She had talent and ambition. She was destined for bigger and better things.

Unlike you, mocked a voice inside Rosie's head.

'A pity,' mused Corso. 'I thought they might have enjoyed seeing the island again.' He fixed her with a curious look. 'Are you looking forward to the ball tonight, Rosie?'

Not really, since I'm certain my dress will stand out like a sore thumb and I'll look like an absolute fright next to some of the other women who are here.

'Of course. Can't wait,' she said, forcing a smile.

Corso repressed a click of irritation, because it was obvious she wasn't speaking the truth and he found that disappointing, because hadn't he always thought that Rosie Forrester was completely straightforward? It had been one of the things he'd most liked about her.

The last time he'd seen her she had been gangly and ungainly—and unfortunately, she still was. There had been no transformation or blossoming in the intervening years, as so often happened to women in the time between adolescence and womanhood. Her legs were still long and skinny—her knees as knobbly as a teenage boy's. She was the only woman on the beach without the adornment of jewellery and if you factored in her plain swimsuit and unflattering straw hat, she was someone you noticed for all the wrong reasons. Yet for a moment, Corso found himself admiring her refusal or inability to conform to an invitation to today's picnic which had read: *Beach party chic.*

He wondered if it had been a mistake to invite her. When her father had finally died last year, he had wanted to reach out to offer the family more comfort than a formal letter of condolence. But he hadn't known how and, naturally, there was the thorny issue of royal protocol to consider. The relationship between him and the Forrester family had always been too imprecise to fall into any recognisable category, but his own father had been unequivocal when Corso had brought the matter to his attention.

'Lionel Forrester is dead,' the King had announced, with the dismissive attitude he applied to everyone, including his own son. Corso gave the ghost of a smile. *Especially* his own son. 'And yes, he was the greatest archaeologist Monterosso has ever known and a good teacher to you, but our association with his family is now at an end. The palace has paid the school fees for his two daughters and provided a generous stipend for his widow. We can do nothing more for them, Corso, nor should we.'

But Corso had disagreed. To the King's anger, he had invited Rosie, Bianca and their mother to his birthday ball, thinking it would be an enormous treat for them to revisit the country after so long—something to tell their friends about back in England. After all, how many commoners were invited to stay in one of Europe's most lavish royal palaces and be entertained by a crown prince?

He had imagined gratitude and a satisfactory sense of closure. He certainly hadn't expected two refusals in rapid succession—and for the only attendee to be a sulky-looking teenager who looked as if she were being subjected to a particular type of torture.

'Try to look as if you mean it, Rosie,' he advised acidly. 'Most people would kill to go to one of my balls.'

'Let's hope not. I'd hate to witness any form of homicide on your birthday,' she answered, with a sudden return of her customary spirit. 'And I think someone over there is trying to get your attention.'

A touch impatiently—for he did not care for flippancy *or* her sudden change of subject—Corso turned his head to follow the direction of her gaze and saw one of the most beautiful women he'd ever laid eyes on heading their way. Tiffany Sackler, with her flawless skin and all that long, dark hair which tumbled to her tiny waist. A small smile edged his lips as she sashayed across the sand towards them, a pair of sunglasses perched provocatively on the end of her nose.

As well as her very obvious physical attributes, the brunette had played hard to get from the moment he'd met her. This was rare enough to excite his interest—despite him never doubting that it was anything other than a game on her part—for Corso was familiar with the plotting of women. And although Tiffany's occupation as one of the world's best-paid supermodels meant she was popular tabloid fodder, her arrival on Monterosso had been as discreet as he could have wished for, which was another point in her favour. Her credentials as a prospective lover were therefore impeccable, which left only one question in Corso's mind.

Did he want her?

He felt the beat of something like indecision before ruthlessly eradicating it. Yes, of course he wanted her. He had been spending far too much time on affairs of state lately, as he prepared himself for his eventual accession to the throne. He wondered if his appetite for women had simply become jaded the more avidly he was pursued—as had happened for most of his life. Yet surely it was a sad day when a man allowed work or caution to subdue his legendary libido. And since he was determined to follow his father's example of enjoying a long and faithful marriage, then surely it only made sense to sow his wild oats before that day came around.

A slow rush of breath escaped from his lungs. Tonight, he decided. After the ball was over. That would be the perfect time to take Tiffany Sackler to his bed.

'Tiffany,' he murmured. 'Good to see you.'

'I'd… I'd better go.' Rosie's voice broke into his thoughts and he realised he'd forgotten she was still there. He turned to see that her cheeks were the colour of a morning sunrise.

'Goodbye, Your Royal Highness,' she added, bobbing another awkward curtsey to him, before grabbing an ugly-looking beach bag and rushing away across the sand before he could stop her or give her permission to leave. Not that he had any intention of stopping her, but still—she should have known better than to go before he had dismissed her.

He frowned.

A man was only a true man if he was able to acknowledge his mistakes and Corso saw now that he definitely should *not* have invited her. The boundaries between them had become blurred. The sunny child he remembered had been replaced by an awkward and self-conscious young woman, who was no longer comfortable mixing in royal circles. Rosie Forrester had no place here—that much was glaringly obvious. His jaw tightened in a moment of exasperation, but at least there were only a few more hours for her to get through before she boarded her flight back to England.

Because the sooner she was away from Monterosso, the better.

Rosie didn't stop rushing until she was back in the grounds of the palace and the crushed diamond glitter of the beach was far behind her. Skirting the less used paths she knew so well, she was able to move unseen through the fragrant foliage, towards the turreted creamy patina of the soaring royal residence. And it wasn't until she was safely back in her room and had closed the door behind her that she drew in a shuddering breath of relief.

And anger.

She found herself staring into an enormous mirror without really seeing herself, because the only things which dominated her thoughts were those piercing amber eyes which gleamed like purest gold.

Had Corso *always* been so hateful? First of all he'd looked her up and down with faint incredulity and then started behaving as if she were invisible—while his jaw had practically dropped to the ground when Tiffany Sackler had appeared with that foxy look on her face. As soon as the supermodel had arrived, the whole atmosphere had changed, making Rosie grow increasingly uncomfortable. Or was she just being naïve and unrealistic? What had she expected? That the Prince would prefer to talk to her, when one of the most lusted-after women on the planet was in the vicinity, batting her super-long lashes at him?

But of all the women he could have had—why choose Tiffany? Or was it her own lack of self-esteem which made Rosie suspicious of the American model, whose eyes she thought resembled shards of blue ice? Her suite was right door next to hers and, since the thick palace walls meant the phone signal was hopeless, Tiffany would sometimes wander out onto her terrace, wearing an eye-poppingly tiny bikini, chattering into her phone and surveying the magnificent scenery around her with a hungry expression. Surely Corso could have found himself a less *in your face* girlfriend than that?

But his relationship with Tiffany was nothing to do with her and Rosie forced herself to focus on the pale face which was staring back at her from the ornately scrolled mirror. She needed to get things in perspective. Tonight was the Prince's birthday ball and after that the clock would start ticking down towards her departure. Just a few more hours to get through and then she could fly back to England and decide what she was going to do with her future.

But the future was scary. She knew that better than anyone. Thank heavens no one was ever given a crystal ball, because if you knew some of the things which were waiting for you—you'd never get out of bed in the morning. She hoped that her mother would start becoming the warm, loving woman she'd grown up with, rather than the pale and haunted widow who seemed unable to cope with her husband's death.

In an effort to distract herself from reality, Rosie began flicking through the bookshelf until she found a book she recognised. A record of early Monterossian art, written by the man who had introduced her to the subject almost before she could walk. The man who had been her hero and the lynchpin on whom the three Forrester women had depended—perhaps a little too much—until his spirit and body had been crushed by an underwater arch which had collapsed on him. The density of the water had meant he hadn't been killed instantly, as would have happened if it had occurred on dry land. Instead, he had lain in a coma for four long years before his eventual death, which had given the family time to reflect on the fact that

Lionel's enthusiasm had stupidly led him to undertake a dangerous mission, single-handedly. It had been a slow kind of suffering for them all—and now his work and his two daughters were all that remained of him.

It had been a long time since Rosie had been able to bring herself to look at this particular book, but it was comforting as well as poignant to read the familiar words, for it conjured up her father's voice and his presence. Lost in tales of ancient battles and of jewelled crowns forged for royal princesses, Rosie was oblivious to the hours drifting by until she heard a noise coming from the direction of Tiffany's terrace. With a shock, she glanced down at her watch and realised there was barely an hour left before the ball began. She hadn't even thought about getting ready—and no way should she be late.

A quick shower washed all the remaining sand from her body but there wasn't enough time to wash and dry her hair. Never mind. She could twist it into an intricate knot, high on her head, and hopefully that would conceal the fact that some of the strands were still covered in suncream. At last she plucked her dress from the ornately carved wardrobe, her heart hammering nervously as she pulled it over her head.

'*Keep it simple,*' her sister had advised, and,

since Bianca always looked totally amazing, Rosie had taken her at her word. She suspected that the only reason she'd been able to afford the dress was because the unforgiving white fabric would have revealed every lump and bump on most people, of which Rosie had none. The gown was silky and fell to the ground, pretty much covering her feet—which was a good thing as she was wearing a pair of red ballet pumps which still fitted her and which she had never really used, since she'd always been hopeless at dancing. She still was. The most daring thing about the outfit was that it draped over one shoulder, leaving the other completely bare. Her only adornment was a delicate choker of gold, a replica of an ancient Monterossian necklace which her mother had lent her. But the catch was fiddly and Rosie's fingers much too nervous to secure it…

Couldn't she go and ask Tiffany to fasten it for her? Forget her prejudices about the American supermodel and perhaps have a friendly chat with her before the big event. Wasn't that the companionable kind of thing women sometimes did before parties? Maybe they could even go to the ball together—because that would be infinitely better than having to enter the luxurious palace ballroom on her own.

Her ballet pumps were silent as she crossed the marble floor and she was going to approach from the shadows of her own terrace, when she saw Tiffany standing with her back to her. Her phone was held to her ear and Rosie was just about to retreat and return once the call was finished when her ears pricked up as she heard a name she recognised.

'Oh, don't worry. I have Corso *exactly* where I want him,' Tiffany was purring.

Rosie had been taught never to listen to other people's conversations because nothing good ever came of it, but a faintly troubling quality in the supermodel's voice was making her body grow tense.

Leave, she told herself, but she remained rooted to the spot all the same.

'Because I've made him wait and he's hot for me, and my timing couldn't be more perfect.' Tiffany was whispering, before letting out a soft and triumphant laugh. 'Yes, you do. You know exactly what I mean. And if the stars align themselves properly, you're going to be organising a baby shower before the year is out. Yeah, yeah…'

The rest of her words were lost as Rosie slipped back into her room, her thoughts spinning.

Disbelief washed over her as she thought

about what she'd just heard. Could Tiffany have meant what it *sounded* as if she meant? As if she was planning to trap the Prince by getting herself pregnant? Surely she wouldn't do something as crass and as underhand as that.

But she wouldn't have been the first woman in the history of the world to have stooped to such an action. Rosie might have been completely innocent of men, but she knew that much. Her face grew hot and she wanted to squirm. Because if that *were* the case, then surely she couldn't just remain silent about it, because in essence—that would be condoning it. Did Corso *realise* what was on Tiffany's mind? Did he have any idea what might be waiting in store for him?

Because she knew very well that the Crown Prince had always been a traditionalist and his royal legacy was hugely important to him. And yes, his sexual exploits might give people the idea that he was a playboy, but he was also the type of man who would marry only when the time was right—to a woman of a similar exalted royal background. He certainly wasn't the kind of man who would have a baby out of wedlock, with a commoner.

Trying to keep her fingers steady, Rosie fiddled with her necklace until at last it was fastened and she wished she could just crawl underneath the embroidered covers of the magnificent bed and sleep the night away until her flight home tomorrow. But she couldn't do that. She couldn't.

What *should* she do?

She swallowed.

She and Corso went back a long way—even if he *had* been unable to conceal his faint disdain for her today or the fact that, inevitably, they had grown apart. And anyway, this was about more than her own hurt pride. Surely she owed it to the Prince, to his land and his people to confide in him the truth. She *had* to tell him. Before it was too late.

She heard the first of eight sonorous clangs as the palace clock began to ring in the hour.

Despite all her best intentions, she was late.

The final chime was just dying away as Rosie burst into the ballroom to confront the Crown Prince of Monterosso.

CHAPTER TWO

SITTING BENEATH THE glittering chandeliers which hung from the vaulted ceiling of the ballroom, Corso did his best to stifle another yawn. The lavish birthday feast was almost over and as soon as the cake had been cut, the dancing could begin. And not a moment too soon, in his opinion. Why the hell had he agreed to celebrate his quarter-century with a glittering party? Had he forgotten that these affairs could feel interminably long, as well as tediously predictable? Forcing his expression into one of benign approval, he nodded as an enormous cake was wheeled into the ballroom and the entire room burst into song.

He could feel the heat from the candle flames as the extravagant concoction reached him and, with one mighty expulsion of air, he leaned forward to extinguish them, to the accompaniment of rapturous applause. With an air of apparent enjoyment, he took a mouthful of wild strawberry and cream gateau and washed it down with a sip of vintage champagne, but afterwards pushed the plate and the glass away. It occurred to Corso that for each year that passed, he enjoyed his birthday less and less.

During the banquet itself, he had sat between two high-born women from neighbouring countries—a countess and a duchess—but this had solely been a nod to propriety. A reassurance to his father—who was not present—and to the courtiers who feared he wasn't giving proper consideration to his future and, more importantly, an heir. And you could not have an heir without first finding a royal wife to bear him.

But the women had bored him, as they so often did. Corso had not been dazzled by their perfect manners, nor their jewels. He certainly hadn't been tempted by their coy references to the bloated coffers of each of their kingdoms. Presumably intimating at the large dowry which could be his, should he request either of their hands in marriage, for in this part of the world tradition still prevailed. He knew that when the time came, he would take a wife of a noble lineage which resembled his own and he was okay with that. It was just the way things were and he had long ago accepted his destiny.

But this evening he had been far more interested in observing Tiffany Sackler busily chatting with the handsome man on her right and not looking in Corso's direction once. Several times she had thrown back her head and laughed, as if her companion were the single most amusing person in the world. Yet her actions had irritated him and her evident game-playing had quelled a little of the hunger in his blood.

A sudden movement caught his attention and he looked down the far end of the banqueting table to see Rosie Forrester staring at him, chewing her bottom lip as if she were worried about something. Her eyes looked huge and she was pursing her lips together, as if trying to silently convey something to him. As their gaze met, she half lifted her arm to wiggle her forefinger at him in a wave and Corso expelled a sigh of irritation.

What was the *matter* with the girl?

First, she had arrived after everyone else— bursting into the ballroom all out of breath. To have been late at the birthday party of the Prince of Monterosso was bad enough, but her social gaffe was compounded by the fact that she was wearing what appeared to be a repurposed bedsheet. He had stared in brief amazement at the silky white material which had skimmed her slender frame, unable to miss the crimson ballet shoes exposed by the flying fabric. With its one-shouldered nod to a Grecian goddess, she had looked as if she were going to a downmarket fancy-dress party. And now she was trying to get his attention! Wasn't she aware that her behaviour was totally out of line? Very deliberately, Corso turned away from her and began to speak to his aide, Rodrigo, who had appeared by his side and was enquiring about the commencement of the dancing.

'Let the music begin,' Corso said, with a swift inclination of his head. The violins began to play as he rose to his feet, the orchestra not quite managing to drown out the collective holding of breath as the assembled gathering waited to see which woman he would choose to open the dancing. He was aware that his choice of partner was significant, knowing if he selected either the countess or the duchess then the media would go wild and wedding-dress manufacturers would be giving non-stop interviews to the broadcast media tomorrow morning.

He observed that by now Tiffany's eyes *were*

on him but, still irritated by her game-playing, he decided to let her wait and fret for a moment or two, before walking over to where she sat and extending his hand.

'Would you do me the honour?' he questioned carelessly.

Her curtsey was deep and practised and she held the submissive pose just long enough for him to get ample exposure to the creamy swell of her cleavage, which no doubt had been her intention. 'I would be delighted, Your Royal Highness,' she replied huskily.

The guests made a circle around them as they began to move in time to the music and Tiffany began to talk, as if determined to make the most of this rare public one-to-one with the Crown Prince. Corso listened while she prattled away in her sultry drawl, extolling the virtues of his country, the magnificence of the view from her suite of rooms and the lavishness of the meal she had just eaten. Her body was light yet strong and she was an accomplished dancer. He could feel the occasional brush of her erect nipples against his chest, as he was certain he was meant to, and it had the desired effect of arousing him. Yet he felt curiously…*detached*, and he frowned.

Maybe a bout of energetic sex would cure him of his ennui.

'I will see you later,' he promised, his voice growing husky.

She looked up at him with teasing provocation in her blue eyes. 'Oh, really?'

'*Si... certo,*' he murmured, lapsing into Italian, rather than his native tongue. 'But for now I must play fair and give other women the chance to dance with me, or I will have a riot on my hands.'

'I understand perfectly, Your Royal Highness. Until *later*, then.' She bowed her gleaming head and dropped another graceful curtsey, before retreating in a swish of lavishly embroidered silk.

Corso began what he thought of as his duty, working his way through as many of the female guests as possible. He saw their expressions of joy, of hope, and the pure delight which greeted his invitation to dance and knew that the majority of them longed to be his bride. Who could blame them? He was young and virile and had been told more times than he could count just how devastating sexy women found him. That he was heir to one of the most wealthy kingdoms on the planet only increased his worth in the eyes of the opposite sex.

Towards the tail end of the evening, he supposed he really ought to partner young Rosie in a duty dance but when he looked to find her, she was nowhere to be seen. More champagne was poured and an ensemble of acrobats from Monterosso's leading circus performed a series of awe-inspiring routines, in dramatic costumes which resembled flames. Finally, everyone moved out onto the wide veranda to engage in a little stargazing before the firework display, which was timed to start at exactly midnight, the official end of the Crown Prince's birthday.

But just as Corso was preparing to take his place at the front of the balustrade, he felt something tugging at his sleeve. Or rather, someone. With a scowl, he looked down to discover who'd had the temerity to touch him in such a fashion—knowing that if Tiffany was attempting to draw attention to their proposed liaison, then she would be history before they'd even begun—when he saw Rosie looking up at him.

In her bedsheet dress she looked even paler than usual and strands of hair from her updo—although admittedly a magnificent shade of moonlight—remained wild. It looked as if she'd been running anxious fingers through it all evening, which, judging from her expression, was

entirely possible. Her only jewellery was a replica of an ancient Monterossian necklace—the
beaten metal gleaming softly against her milky
skin. And something about that simple choker
made Corso's equilibrium falter for a moment.
She was no match for the society guests here
tonight, he thought, yet her careless appearance caused a peculiar awareness to shimmer
through his body, which made him feel decid-
edly *disconcerted*. It whispered featherlight
fingers over his flesh. It hinted at something
delicious and unknown. But it was gone almost
as soon as he had acknowledged it, banished
by a swift shake of his head.

'Corso,' she whispered.

Now she was addressing him without waiting
for his permission to speak—and in a highly in-
subordinate manner! 'What is it?' he snapped.

'I need to talk to you.'

'Well, you can't.'

'But—'

'Not only is your request highly inappropriate,' he bit out, from between gritted teeth, 'but
it is also untimely. In case you hadn't noticed,
this happens to be my birthday party and there
are many guests craving my attention. Princes
and sheikhs who have travelled many miles to
be here, as well as many old friends.'

'But I need to speak to you,' she said, with an oddly stubborn note in her voice. 'I'll never forgive myself if I don't.'

Scarcely able to believe her audacity, Corso considered his options. If he sent her away there would be a scene and, besides, the mulish expression pinned to her face made him doubt she would obey him—he had never seen her look that way before. What was the *matter* with her? Having her removed by Security remained an option, of course, but the forced removal of a troublesome guest was hardly an auspicious end to his party—and would doubtless cause gossip and speculation. And since this was doubtless the last time he would ever see her, why not tolerate her request and hear her out?

Knitting his brows together, he glanced up at the illuminated dial of the mighty clock as the hour ticked irrevocably towards midnight. Would five minutes be long enough to allow her to get whatever it was off her chest before he dismissed her?

He dipped his head so his words couldn't be overheard, their silky tone failing to disguise his irritation. 'Very well. I will grant you a few minutes. What is it?'

Rosie hesitated, glancing this way and that, terrified someone would be able to hear what she was about to say. 'Not here,' she whispered. 'Can't we just go over there, where it's quiet?'

'No.'

'Yes, we can, Corso,' she persisted stubbornly. 'You're the most senior royal here tonight. You can do anything you please.'

'Good to know that you're able to remember protocol when it suits you,' he answered testily.

But to her relief, he waved away the aides who were hovering anxiously nearby and strode over to the velvet-curtained recess she'd indicated, where indigo shadows replaced the bright glitter of the ballroom, and Rosie followed him—steeling herself against the fierce look on his face.

'Well? What is it?' he demanded. 'I'm waiting.'

But now that the moment of revelation was here, Rosie couldn't work out how she was going to say it, because this was something way outside her experience. Way outside most people's, she guessed uncomfortably. How did you tell any man—let alone a hugely important royal—that you thought someone was attempting to trick them in the most underhand way possible?

'It's Tiffany,' she said, at last.

He stilled. 'Tiffany?'

Rosie nodded. 'That's right.'

'What about her?'

'I don't think… I don't think she has your best interests at heart.'

'No?' He gave a short, disbelieving laugh. 'But you do, I suppose?'

Again, she hesitated as the hard light from his eyes lanced through her. 'Yes, I do. Of course I do.'

'So what is it about her which makes you think I should be on my guard?' he questioned sarcastically. 'Surely you're not jealous that I had the first dance with her and didn't find time to dance with you? Is that why your eyes were following me round the ballroom so reproachfully all evening?'

Rosie froze. Did he really think this was about *jealousy*—or imagine he was so gorgeous that all a woman could think about was craving his company? She was so outraged by his assumption that she nearly turned on her heel and fled, because it would serve him right if he created a love child with Tiffany Sackler on the very night of his twenty-fifth birthday. And then a feeling of nausea rose up inside her as she acknowledged her own dated terminology. *Love child?* Nobody said that sort of thing any more. What if she *had* got it all wrong? She had zero experience of sex, or relationships. What if she'd misread the situation and was sticking her nose in where it wasn't needed? For all she knew, he and Tiffany might already have had long and avid discussions about planned parenthood. She had read the textbooks at school, along with everyone else. Who was to say they hadn't spent the last three days taking her temperature and deciding which would be the best sexual position to adopt?

Her fingers strayed to her lips because that particular thought made her feel queasy and she wasn't quite sure why. But the Prince's eyes were narrowed with exasperation and she thought he was about to stride away and she'd never get another chance. Maybe it was that which made it all come tumbling out, her words almost tripping over themselves. 'I don't want to be the one to have to tell you this, Corso, but Tiffany and I have suites next door to each other. Our terraces are connected and I overheard her talking on the phone earlier.'

'You mean you were eavesdropping?'

'Yes. No.' She shook her head, knowing that she probably deserved the withering disdain she could hear in his voice and knowing she needed to justify it. 'I never intended to stay and listen but then I heard… I heard her talking to someone—'

'That is usually what happens when you're on the phone to someone,' he interrupted sarcastically.

'And she was saying…' She shrugged her shoulders with helpless embarrassment. 'She was saying that she'd made you wait and you were hot for her. And…'

A sudden chill seemed to have entered the atmosphere. 'And?'

Rosie could see that his face had changed. The irritation had vanished and been replaced by a look of cold, quiet danger.

For a moment she questioned the wisdom of what she was about to do, but somehow she knew there wasn't any other choice. Because not only was Rosie spurred on by the certainty that the da Vignola lineage was too long and revered a line to be continued in such a potentially destabilising way, there was another factor, too. No way should Corso Andrea da Vignola become a parent. Certainly not at this stage in his life—perhaps not ever. Because how could a man ever raise a child when he was so proud and unfeeling and downright arrogant?

'She said it was perfect timing.'

'Perfect timing?' he repeated slowly.

It occurred to Rosie that his innate superiority might prevent him from understanding the harsh truth of what she was telling him. He probably imagined that any woman would think it perfect timing to have the royal Prince in their bed and that she, for all her innocence, had misunderstood what Tiffany had been alluding to. So enlighten him—even if it's the most embarrassing thing you've ever had to do.

'She said something about there being a possible baby shower before the year was out,' she whispered. 'I got the feeling that was what she meant. That she wanted to…that she wanted to have your baby.'

A ragged breath erupted from his lungs. It sounded like a caged beast breaking free and Rosie had to concentrate very hard not to take an instinctive step back. She had seen Corso many times during her life—admittedly only through the eyes of someone who was young and untutored—but she had never seen him look anything like this before. Naked fury darkened his brilliant eyes, followed by a spiky glint of anger. She wondered if he was going to thank her for telling him before it was too late, but maybe that was naïve because there was nothing resembling gratitude on his hard features. He looked utterly magnificent but also utterly terrifying.

Don't shoot the messenger, she wanted to say, but of course—she didn't dare.

He was nodding his head, like someone doing sums inside their head, before coming to some kind of calculation. His words were slow and measured. 'This is the beginning and the end of this conversation. Do not ever speak of it again. Not to anyone,' he instructed. 'Believe me, I will know if you have broken this confidence and I will make you pay. Do you understand what I'm saying to you, Rosie?'

She nodded. He was asking her to keep this a secret. To collude with him.

She thought how differently he could have put it. He could have made it sound like a strengthening bond between them, but it was nothing like that. His words were a warning—maybe even a threat. As if the already wide chasm which existed between them had opened up even wider. As if he were standing on the deck of a giant ocean liner which was moving slowly but irrevocably away from her.

And she should not forget that he had also insulted her. He'd accused her of jealousy. Of mooning around and being somehow offended because he hadn't asked her to dance.

As if! She'd rather scrub the palace floor with a toothbrush than dance with *him*. Somehow she couldn't imagine ever seeing him again after tonight, let alone speaking to him. And wouldn't that be for the best? To finally put Monterosso and all its bittersweet memories behind her. To forget that once she had eaten chicken pie with a crown prince, and try to get on with the rest of her life, wherever that took her?

'Yes, Your Royal Highness,' she emphasised sarcastically, but her formal acknowledgement of his title must have reassured him that she meant what she said, because he nodded with patriarchal acceptance.

'Good. I think that is all. And now, if you will excuse me, people are expecting fireworks and I must signal for them to begin.'

And that was that. No thanks. No further acknowledgement. Nothing but a cool gaze before the Prince swept out from within the curtained recess. After a couple of moments Rosie did the same and watched as he walked towards the front of the palace balustrade, and people parted to clear a path for him, as they always did. She could see Tiffany glancing towards him as he lifted his hand in command for the fireworks to begin.

But he did not look in Tiffany's direction. Not once. Rosie saw a trace of discomposure cross the supermodel's exquisite features, just as Corso brought his hand down with the rapid and irreversible movement of a guillotine blade.

As the palace clock struck midnight, fireworks exploded and Monterosso was lit up with silver and pink, with green and blue and crimson. The colours splintered the dark blue sky like bright, kaleidoscopic comets but as the chimes began to die away, Rosie could hear the sound of boots coming towards them...and they were running.

Running.

She knew something was wrong the instant she saw the marble-white faces of the King's inner guard as they sped towards Corso, who was regarding them impenetrably—though in the moonlight she thought she could see the dawning of comprehension hardening those rugged features. And suddenly Rosie guessed what was happening as, to a man, the guard sank to their knees before him, their solemn pronouncement echoing through the shocked silence of the partygoers.

'The King is dead!'

And then.

'Long live the King!'

Corso's strained features reflected the enormity of what was taking place and Rosie wondered if she had imagined the bitter acceptance which briefly darkened his extraordinary eyes.

CHAPTER THREE

Seven years later

THE WOOD WAS dark and dense and it was easy for Corso to remain concealed as he waited for her, beneath the shaded canopy of leaves. There was nobody else around, he had insisted on that—despite the words of warning and handwringing on behalf of his security people. There were guards stationed discreetly throughout the woodland—that much he had conceded—but he had been afforded the privacy he wanted, because he was the King, and in the end everyone always did what the King wanted.

Would it be contrary of him to wish that sometimes they wouldn't?

The woodland was quiet. Everything was quiet, save for the rustle of a nearby squirrel, or the whisper of the breeze in the leaves overhead. There was a sense of green and sylvan

calm, for this was England and it felt a long way
from the warm beaches of Monterosso. Yet it
was curiously life-enhancing to be completely
on his own in a foreign country—for solitude
had become an almost forgotten luxury since
he had inherited the throne, along with so much
else. A deep breath escaped his lungs. Was he
imagining the brief sense of peace which had
washed over him as he had walked through
the forest towards Rosie's cottage, or was that
simply wishful thinking? A brief moment of
anonymity seducing him into thinking that a
better life existed than the one he had.

His mouth hardened. Because didn't everyone think that, to some degree? Surely the fan-
tasy of the unknown had always been more
seductive than the demands of the here and
now.

The sudden cry of startled birds scattering
from the treetops warned him of someone's approach and Corso tensed as, several minutes
later, he saw a figure on a bicycle weaving its
way along the uneven path towards the cottage.

It could only be Rosie but he would never
have recognised her—not in a million years—
and not just because her skinny shape had filled
out. A safety helmet was crammed down over

her head and she wore dark and unprepossessing clothes.

He wondered what her reaction would be when she saw him, and whether she would approve of this covert method of contacting her. He supposed he could have picked up the phone, but instinct had urged him to choose an element of surprise—because in many ways he knew her well enough to break with convention, and wasn't there something *exhilarating* about such an unorthodox approach? Usually his timetable was calculated right down to the precise second and the rigid regimentation of his life inevitably made him feel constrained. But not so today. Today he was master of his own destiny.

Plus, he suspected she wouldn't exactly be overjoyed at seeing him again after their last meeting—particularly as his dramatic accession to the throne meant he hadn't spoken to her since. And that state of affairs would probably have continued, if he hadn't realised that Rosie Forrester was the one person who could provide him with what he needed. Some men might have felt a shimmering of doubt about what he was to ask of her, but not Corso—for he was certain that she would bend to his formidable will. Her father had been a loyal man of service—and his daughter was undeniably cast from the same mould.

She dismounted the bike and disappeared inside the humble house and he crunched his way up the path and knocked on the door. A couple of minutes later the door was opened to reveal Rosie Forrester standing staring at him, with disbelief on her face.

He was prepared for her surprise, but not her dislike. That much was evident from the sudden flash of fire in eyes whose colour he had never really noticed before, which was grey. Grey as the wings of the doves which sometimes darkened the skies over Esmelagu, Monterosso's capital city. He felt momentarily startled—as if he had just stumbled on something unexpectedly beautiful—but her shuttered lashes quickly veiled their stormy hue.

'Hello, Rosie,' he said softly.

She was shaking her head. 'I can't...'

'Can't, what?'

'I can't believe it's you.'

At this, he smiled but he noticed she didn't smile back. 'You are surprised I have awarded you such an honour?' he questioned benignly.

'That's not exactly how I would have described it,' she said, before adding, as if she had only just remembered, 'Your *Majesty*.'

Corso felt her unfriendliness crash over him in almost tangible waves and he narrowed his eyes, because such a reaction was rare. Even if they hated him—as he was sure many did— his position always daunted people. Thus, they presented what they thought he wanted from them. Grovelling and deference were high on this list—usually delivered in obscene amounts, which sometimes amused him—because those who fawned over him clearly had no idea just how much such an attitude bored him. But Rosie clearly had no such ambition to impress him. Her lips remained set in a mulish line and Corso's brow knitted together for women never reacted to him this way. He was used to provocation. To guile and glamour. Perhaps it was down to the awkwardness of their last conversation when diplomacy and convention had been eroded by her startling disclosure about Tiffany, and he shuddered now to think how careless he had been up until that night.

But that experience had been a wake-up call and perhaps he should be grateful to her for enlightening him. Alongside his sudden accession to the throne, Rosie's revelation had changed him. Hardened him. Made him acknowledge there were few people in this world you could trust. His mouth twisted. But it had also made him better able to withstand the even more bitter truths which had been hovering in the background like malignant forces. Unpalatable facts just waiting for him, once he had begun to delve into the late King's affairs.

And ultimately, that was what had brought him here today.

Once again, he smiled. 'I would like to talk to you,' he said.

But she seemed oblivious to any kind of charm offensive, or indeed to the unthinkable reality that he remained standing on the doorstep, like a cold-call salesman! And now she was peering suspiciously over his shoulder.

'Where is everyone? Your security detail? The armoured car and the heavy mob? The men with suspicious bulges in their jackets?'

'They are present, but concealed throughout the woods. There's no need to worry about my safety, Rosie.'

'It's not your safety I'm worried about, Corso—it's my privacy.'

'Your privacy?'

'Yes.' She bit down on her lip, hard. 'I don't want tomorrow morning's papers carrying some kind of cloak and dagger story about a Mediterranean king paying a surprise visit to a quiet English hamlet.'

'King being the operative word and one which you might do well to remember,' he prompted lazily.

Their gazes clashed, and perhaps she responded better to authority than persuasion for she seemed to pull herself up—stepping back within the confines of the small cottage.

'You'd better come in, I suppose.'

'I am bowled over by your enthusiastic invitation,' he drawled sarcastically.

'Nobody's forcing you to come in, Corso,' she said, but so quietly that he almost missed it and, since he wanted something from her, he was prepared to overlook her rudeness.

Dipping his head, Corso entered the cottage, narrowly missing an overhanging beam, straightening up to find himself standing in the smallest room he had ever seen, and he looked around, curious to see how she lived.

Modestly, it would seem. His sources had told him as much but the evidence of his own eyes spoke volumes. The woodland setting of the cottage was perfect, but its interior suggested that money was scarce. A small, battered sofa with shiny arms. On an equally small table—next to her discarded cycling helmet—stood a vase filled with a yellow sunburst of daffodils—a quintessentially English touch.

But it was the vase which captured his attention more than the spring flowers, for it was decorated in different shades of blue—the distinctive pottery for which Monterosso was renowned. One of his country's more wholesome trades, he thought bitterly—before turning his attention to Rosie herself. And now it was his turn to be surprised and not just because she was regarding him with that same unwelcoming stare. She had unzipped her bulky waterproof jacket so that it was flapping open and he found himself taken aback by the glimpse of abundant curves which lay beneath. And Corso swallowed.

What had happened to her?

Gone were the angular lines and skinny ribs of her boyish frame and in their place was the swell of generous bosom, demurely covered in a navy-blue sweater on which was embroidered a tiny red logo of a train. Her legs—once bony—were now slender and shapely, despite the workmanlike fabric of her trousers. But it wasn't just her physical appearance which had changed. This was a Rosie he didn't recognise, for the look on her face was almost…*insolent*.

She would never have looked at him like that before yet somehow her defiance was heating his blood. He could feel the sudden quickening of his pulse and his mind began to stir with forgotten memories of how delicious sex could be, before he curtailed his errant thoughts. Hadn't he embraced celibacy for the last seven years, ruthlessly sublimating his healthy libido with hard work and exercise? It had been a long time since he had allowed the warm curl of lust to fire his blood and that was the way he had wanted it.

So why the hell was he thinking this way about someone as unsuitable as Rosie Forrester?

His throat dried.

Because denial created hunger. And in the end, wouldn't a starving man sooner devour the hunk of dry bread lying on the table before him, than hold out for a banquet which might never materialise?

So dial it down. Be pleasant. Formal. Remind her—and yourself—of the natural order of things. 'How are you, Rosie?' he questioned, with the same polite distance he might use if he were greeting someone standing in the official line during the opening of a sardine factory.

'Honestly? I'm confused. Bewildered, even.' She shrugged. 'If you must know, I'm wondering why you're here. Why the King of Monterosso has turned up on my doorstep without any kind of warning.'

Corso frowned. Shouldn't she be displaying a little more excitement than this? He had been expecting to have been offered a very English cup of tea—which he would almost certainly have refused—and to have been invited to sit on one of the uncomfortable-looking pieces of furniture. He hadn't been anticipating this cool reception on her part, despite the awkwardness of their last meeting.

She had changed, he thought, before wondering why he'd ever thought otherwise. Of course she had.

They had all changed.

His mouth hardened.

Seven years was a long time.

'I need a favour,' he said.

Rosie was careful to keep her expression neutral, though inside she wasn't feeling a bit like that—and for once it wasn't worry about her mother, or fear of the future which was making her pulse race. An unfamiliar sense of disorientation was unsettling her and it had nothing to do with the shock of protocol being blown away by the King's surprise appearance. It had nothing to do with his lofty position in the world and everything to do with the man himself.

Because Corso Andrea da Vignola had somehow acquired the ability of making the humble dimensions of her cottage shrink even further. It felt as if the walls had started closing in on her. She was finding it difficult to breathe, or think, or concentrate. It was impossible to look anywhere other than at him, yet she had no desire to look anywhere else.

Her gaze drank in the angled planes of his sculpted features and aristocratic cheekbones, as if she needed to commit them to memory. The arrogant curve of his sensual lips and metallic blaze of his eyes. She'd always been aware that his body was strong and powerful—his physical prowess was legendary—but suddenly it wasn't easy to be quite so objective about it. With a sudden flash of insight, Rosie understood why women used to swoon whenever he was around. Why their faces would contort with desire when they thought he wasn't looking.

Her heart skipped an uncomfortable beat. Had she too fallen victim to his allure after years of being immune to it? Was she fated to join the bloated ranks of women who desired him, who humiliated themselves in their desire to get him to bed them, or wed them?

She gave herself a mental shake. No, she was not. Only a fool would wander down that path. She needed an urgent encounter with reality and to remember their last encounter, when all traces of the old Corso seemed to have vanished. He had been cold and cruel, accusing her of jealousy when she'd told him what she'd overheard. He had looked her up and down as if she were something unpleasant he'd found clinging to the sole of his boots. And then he'd dismissed her—making her feel small and inconsequential—before the night had descended into total chaos. His father had died unexpectedly and Corso had been pronounced King, right before her eyes. The ball had ended abruptly and the whole country had been plunged into mourning.

On her flight back to England the next day, Rosie had wondered if Corso had gone ahead and spent the night with Tiffany anyway, because hadn't she read somewhere that people found comfort in sex, during times of intense grief? But if he had, there had been no apparent consequences. No baby and certainly no wedding. Tiffany Sackler had gone on to marry some hedge-fund manager and was living between Manhattan and the Hamptons. And if occasionally Rosie had seen articles about Corso in newspapers, which took great pains to report that he remained resolutely single, she genuinely hadn't cared.

She needed to remember that she was a different person now. She was seven years older and had cut her ties with him and his homeland completely. She had grown up—in all ways. Physically, she had been a late developer, but at twenty, her body had suddenly filled out. Almost overnight she'd stopped being skinny and gawky and had acquired curves and she'd had to get used to having breasts, and hips. She had found a job she enjoyed, even if it didn't pay quite as much as she would like. But she supplemented her income with extra work *and* she was almost at the end of a perfectly respectable online arts degree, even though she hadn't been able to utilise it yet. She had made something of herself and didn't have to hang onto his every word, or agree with him, or bow down to him. She didn't even have to talk to him if she didn't want to. She wasn't his subject and she owed him nothing.

Nothing. Not even the cowering deference which he probably thought was his due.

'I did you a favour once before and you threw it back in my face,' she reminded him.

'That was wrong of me.' He hesitated, like a person who was about to use unfamiliar phraseology. 'I was—am—very grateful to you.'

Her gaze was suspicious. 'Really?'

'Really.' His words were dry. 'Unfortunately, you didn't choose the most opportune moment to tell me.'

'It was the only one I had. I couldn't get near you all evening, or work my way through the adoring crush.' The unreasonable accusations of jealousy he had thrown at her had rankled for a long time, and Rosie subjected him to a steady stare. 'Anyway, that's all in the past. I'm puzzled why you think I could do you a favour, Corso. What possible use can I be when you're one of the best-connected men in the world while I am just an ordinary woman?'

'Perhaps that is the key to your usefulness,' he mused. 'The sheer ordinariness of your life.' His rich gaze seared over her. 'Forgive me if my words offend you.'

'Why should they?' she questioned, though of course—they did. 'Like me, you are only stating facts.'

'Indeed. You have a job on the railways, I understand?'

Did he really? Rosie wondered acidly. Could a man in his position ever *understand* what it was like to work for a living, or worry about where his next meal was coming from?

She nodded. 'I'm in charge of the catering trolley on the long-distance line which operates between Paddington and Cornwall.' She stabbed her finger against the little red train logo above her breast. 'This is my uniform, in case you were wondering.'

'Indeed.' He inclined his head. 'I confess I was surprised when they told me. It isn't the profession I would have mapped out for you.'

Instinctively, Rosie's eyes narrowed. He must want something very badly if he was prepared to indulge in meaningless small talk like this. 'Is that so?' she questioned innocently. 'What did you imagine me doing, Corso? I'm sure you must have given the matter a good deal of thought over the years.'

His brows narrowed, as if correctly sensing sarcasm. 'Something to do with antiquities, perhaps,' he suggested. 'Or with art, or literature—fine-tuning the gifts you might have inherited from your father. Didn't you used to help him? I often used to see the two of you dusting and polishing precious artefacts around the palace?'

She felt vulnerable then and wished she hadn't challenged him. Of *course* she would have loved to have followed Lionel Forrester into his rarefied field of archaeology, but jobs like that were few and far between. And life had had other plans for her, waiting to emerge from the shadows, like spectres. Those same spectres swept into her mind now and she thought about the constant nag of debt. Of bankruptcy. Of human frailty and the depths to which someone would sink in their pursuit of love. A terrible sadness pierced her heart and it took a moment or two before she trusted herself to speak. 'Yes, I used to help him in school holidays. He taught me all about Monterosso and its rich history and I was very grateful for that. Actually, I've been doing an online arts degree.'

'So I understand.'

'Your people found that out for you as well, did they?'

He shrugged. 'That's what I pay them for.'

'I've submitted my dissertation,' she explained, not quite knowing why she was telling him all this, other than the fact that—amazingly—he actually looked as if he were interested. 'I just haven't had the final degree yet.'

'Which is why I am here today,' he said. 'If you are prepared to hear me out?'

It was so out of character for Corso to seek permission to speak that for a moment Rosie was startled into silence. She wanted to tell him no. To go away and leave her alone—taking his newly distracting presence with him. But she felt as if she had a duty to listen to what he had to say, because her dad had loved him. He had loved him like the son he'd never had and hadn't she sometimes been jealous of that? And she was curious, too. Of course she was. Who wouldn't be, in her position? 'Very well,' she agreed. 'Why don't you sit down and make yourself comfortable?'

But he didn't sit—as if the concept of comfort was irreconcilable with a place like this. He just continued to stand there, dominating the space around him with his hard and brilliant allure, and suddenly Rosie wanted to be as far away from him as was possible. She took off her bulky jacket and hung it on the back of one of the dining chairs, before perching on it, and from here it was impossible not to study him as she waited for him to speak.

He looked older, she thought—and his air of cynicism seemed even more pronounced. The lines around his lips were deeper and his flame-dark hair was flecked with the occasional strand of silver. His body had always been lean, but never had it looked harder than it did right now. As if he'd spent the last seven years banishing every ounce of softness from his frame. As if he were determined that each muscle should be honed and defined. And although he had clearly made an attempt to dress down in jeans and a dark leather jacket—presumably in an attempt to blend in and look 'normal'—he had failed spectacularly, because his aristocratic lineage radiated from him like a precious aura. He exuded charisma and power and something else. She swallowed. Pure, raw sex appeal—there was no other way to describe it.

Rosie's breasts tightened and she felt the wash of something warm and seductive, slowly unfurling inside her. Her breasts began to grow heavy and prickle at the tips. It was a deliciously distracting feeling and because she liked it too much, she wanted it gone. Unseen on her lap, she clenched her fingers, because she didn't want to think of him this way. She didn't want to think of him in *any* way. She wanted her old immunity back and to be protected from this sudden aching awareness of her neglected body.

'Okay, then. Enlighten me.' She laid her

palms flat on the table, directly in front of the vase of daffodils. 'I'm all ears.'

Corso nodded, momentarily distracted by the gleam of her hair, which was a slightly paler shade than the flowers, before cursing the random nature of his thoughts. What a ridiculous thing to preoccupy him at a time like this!

He forced himself to concentrate.

How much to tell her?

How much did she need to know?

He felt the sudden clench of his heart.

As little as possible.

Because information was power—and right now he needed all the power he could retain. Wasn't that one of his greatest fears—that the knowledge he had acquired spelled danger, not just to him, but to his country? That the past was going to rear its ugly head and impact dramatically on his future and the future of his people?

'Your father was responsible for the discovery of Monterosso's most significant and ancient artefacts,' he said. 'In particular, the jewellery collection of the country's tragic young Queen, who died in childbirth, over four thousand years ago.'

'Do you really think I need to be reminded of that?' she answered quietly. 'When the pursuit of that treasure was responsible for his own untimely death. If…if he hadn't been so keen to get back to that underwater burial chamber a second time and had waited for back-up, he might still be alive today.'

Corso saw the way her face had paled. Heard the pain and sadness in her voice. But he detected accusation, too—trembling at the edge of her words as subtly as a night-time breeze—and his eyes narrowed. Did she hold Monterosso responsible for his death?

'Lionel was a passionate archaeologist, Rosie, and sometimes men like that take risks,' he said, more gently than was usual for him. 'That was the life he chose. A life he loved and thrived on. Which drove him. He was impatient to see what that cave contained, which was why he went in on his own. It may not have been what you or I would have done but it was what he wanted.'

Tears pricked the backs of her eyes as Rosie stared down at her fingers, determined that Corso wouldn't see them, because his words were chipping away at her defences and making her feel…*vulnerable*. And instinct told her it was dangerous to feel that way—especially in front of him. Oh, why had he started talking about all this after so long? Didn't she have enough to deal with, without him reminding her of a time when life had been peachy?

'Yes, I know that,' she said, composing herself before lifting her face to meet his gaze. 'But sometimes it seems as though he died for nothing. The treasures he uncovered have never been seen, or even written about. His discovery seemed to have faded into insignificance, as if it had never happened. As if it didn't matter.'

'My thoughts exactly,' he breathed. 'And the reason I am here today.'

The smile which accompanied his words was disturbing and Rosie couldn't work out why. Because it felt strangely *manipulative*?

Or because it was making her blood slug around her veins, as sweet and heavy as honey?

She blinked. It was almost as if Corso were playing with her, in the way an expert angler played a fish, before bringing it dry and gasping to the shore.

'I want the world to see these jewels and marvel at their splendour,' he continued softly. 'I have a vision for Monterosso's future, Rosie, and the collection will help me achieve that vision. I plan to take it on a whistle-stop tour of Paris, New York and London. Some of the most beautiful cities in the world, which will showcase our finest treasures.' There was a pause before his gaze became shuttered by his thick lashes. 'And I want you to come with me.'

CHAPTER FOUR

THE KING'S SILKEN words shimmered through the confines of her tiny sitting room and Rosie stared at him in disbelief.

'You want to take the Monterossian burial jewels around the world and for *me* to accompany you? I'm sorry, but you've lost me, Corso. Why? I mean, why me?'

He frowned with the exasperation of a man not often required to repeat himself.

'It's simple,' he said, not very patiently.

Rather alarmingly, he pulled out a chair and sat down opposite her at the table, so close that Rosie imagined she could feel the warmth of his breath. Close enough to see the dark amber flecks in his golden eyes. And the faux intimacy made Rosie remember when he'd occasionally appear at the door of her parents' grace-and-favour house in Monterosso, and they would invite him to join them for a fam-

ily meal, soon after his mother had died. Her
own mother had urged Rosie and her sister to
treat the Prince 'normally' and they had been
young and unselfconscious enough to comply.
Rosie remembered sometimes thinking how
alone he had seemed, and her heart had gone
out to him.

But that was an erroneous impression, she
reminded herself fiercely. Corso was the least
lonely person on the planet. He was idolised
and adored and always had been. It was well
known that from the moment he had lain in his
cradle, he had been waited on hand and foot,
for he was the only child of the royal marriage
and a precious son and heir. From the moment
he was born, he'd had only to lift a chubby little
fist and one of his adoring nurses would rush
to his side. It was true that his father had been
away a lot and in the latter years his mother
had been very sick, but day and night he was
surrounded by people, eager to fall in with his
every wish. Which made it even more inexplicable why he had turned up *here*, at her little
cottage deep in the forest. But perhaps it was
her memory of those earlier times which made
her lean back in her chair and humour him.

'Carry on,' she said.

Corso nodded, aware of needing to choose

his words carefully because Rosie wasn't the walkover he'd been expecting. He had anticipated her eagerness to agree with whatever it was he suggested, not for her to survey him with that faint air of scepticism. He was here because, essentially, he trusted her, which meant he could tell her some things. He felt his throat dry. Just not everything.

'When I inherited the Kingdom seven years ago, I had to look at my country with different eyes,' he said. 'As a ruler, rather than an heir— and these positions are very different. I was to discover things which had never been apparent to me before...'

'What kind of things?' she interjected curiously as his words tailed off.

Corso shot her a reprimanding look. He wanted to tell her that *he* would be the giver of information, rather than her attempting to take it from him. But something warned him that if he wanted her to fall in with his wishes, then he needed to be diplomatic. And so he nodded benignly, as if he weren't in the least bit irritated by her interruption.

'My father's way of ruling was not my way, Rosie. And the legacy he left me was not... ideal. Now that I have properly settled into my reign, I intend to do things very differently.'

'A new broom,' she suggested quietly.

'If you like.' He got up from the chair and walked over to the window and stared out at the seemingly impenetrable green of the forest outside, before turning back to see her grey eyes fixed on him. 'I did not realise, until the mantle of the throne came upon me, how much I really loved my country. Or, rather, the country I want it to be. I want to forge a new Monterosso. One which is no longer solely dependent on gambling, or providing a tax haven for questionable sources of income. I want an inward investment for my land, which will benefit my people. High-end eco-tourism, among other things. The tour is to showcase some of the historic culture of the nation, but will also serve as a backdrop for my meetings with business leaders and investors. It will act as a reminder of Monterosso's great history, as well as all the possibilities of a great future.'

There was a pause while she absorbed this, touching her fingers to the ends of her thick plait. But her no-nonsense hairstyle was having precisely the wrong effect on him. He imagined himself loosening it, seeing it falling like pale silk between his fingers, and, as he experienced another jerk of unwanted desire, he scowled.

'There's no need to glare at me like that,

Corso,' she said. 'Because, while all this sounds very commendable, I still fail to see how I can help you. I may *almost* have a degree in art, but I have no real experience of mounting an exhibition. In fact, I don't have any experience at all.'

'You don't need any.' Corso felt his jaw tighten as the image of a face swam into his mind. A face similar to his own. *An unknown half-brother who lived on the other side of the world. A man he had never met nor wanted to meet. But he knew that state of affairs could not continue. He couldn't continue burying his head in the sand and pretending his sibling didn't exist.*

His pulse accelerated. And wasn't that the real reason why he wanted to take the jewels on tour—to conceal a potentially threatening assignation behind a cloak of cultural respectability? He shuttered his eyes as he returned her gaze because Rosie didn't need to know that. His mouth hardened. Perhaps nobody needed to know. 'My historians have collated the entire collection.'

'So take *them* with you.'

'I don't want them. I want you. You're the one who can bring the jewels to life because you are Lionel's daughter—and that will add a personal touch like no other. Your presence will ensure the kind of publicity which is impossible to buy, as well as being a fitting testimonial to your family name. Obviously, there will be challenges. But you are young and have potential.' His gaze swept over her assessingly. 'Naturally, you will need to do something about your appearance.'

'What's the matter with my appearance?' she demanded.

'Nothing. I am sure it's completely appropriate for the life you lead but not...' He paused, speculatively. 'Not for a member of the royal party.'

'Are you *trying* to insult me, Corso?'

'Not at all.' He met the stormy flash of her eyes. 'Would you prefer weaselly words of flattery instead of hearing the truth? Especially when beauty can be such a curse,' he added, his words rough.

'Yet one possessed by every woman you've ever been associated with! Funny that.' She pulled a face. 'Well, I must say that the last thing I imagined on my way back from work this afternoon was to find you here, waiting to make me such an extraordinary offer.'

He gave a reflective smile. 'Which, now that you've heard, you are happy to accept?'

As she met his metallic gaze, Rosie gave herself just long enough to imagine what it might be like if she agreed to his bizarre request. She remembered some of the perks which accompanied involvement with the Monterossian royal family. You never had to wait—not for anything. According to her dad, you always got the best rooms and the best service. People tried to get near you and they were prepared to grovel if they thought you had the ear of the King. But that wasn't her world. It never had been, not really—and it would be dangerous to allow herself to be lured back into it.

Yet it was more than that which made her realise she was going to send Corso away without the answer he desired. Mostly, it was because of the way he was making her feel, which was freaking her out. He was doing it right now, with that lazy smile which was drawing attention to the curve of his lips. She'd never found him in the least bit attractive in the past, but something had happened to make her completely reverse that assessment. Because he wasn't just hot, he was dangerous. Way too dangerous for an innocent like her.

She smiled, trying to refuse as tactfully as possible because he wouldn't like it. He wouldn't like it at all. Well, that was tough. It might do him good if someone actually had the nerve to refuse him. 'Flattered as I am to have been asked,' she said, 'I'm afraid my answer has to be no.'

'Are you serious?'

'I'm very serious.'

'Because?'

'Because I already have a job, Corso. It's decent work,' she added defensively, when she saw the incredulous look in his eyes. 'And it pays me an honest wage. I can't just announce that I'm about to fly off with the King of Monterosso on a whim.'

There was a pause which went on a little too long to be entirely comfortable. 'And there's nothing I can do to change your mind?' he said at last.

'Nothing,' she said firmly.

'Are you quite sure about that, Rosie?' he said, in a voice she'd never heard him use before. 'Because I'm thinking your salary must be very modest and probably not enough for your current needs. Am I right?'

Instinctively, Rosie sat up straight because although the words weren't exactly a *threat*, they were definitely underpinned with something disquieting. 'What does my salary have to do with *you*?'

Corso gave a reluctant sigh as her defiance washed over him and for a moment he felt something close to regret. Because he hadn't wanted to do it like this. He'd hoped she would demonstrate the compliancy which was as familiar to him as the sound of his own heartbeat—of people doing what he wanted them to do, without question.

'Why don't you just think of it in terms of an opportunity?' he questioned silkily. 'The tour would take less than a month. You could request unpaid leave and go back to your job once it's over. If you like, I can easily have my people sort that out for you.'

'How very convenient,' she said faintly.

'Or you might think about leaving the railway altogether and trying something new. I have connections you could utilise. You could use the degree you have worked so hard for,' he continued smoothly. 'And I am prepared to be generous, Rosie. Very generous.' The sum he mentioned provoked an instinctive widening of her grey eyes, but just as quickly the look vanished—to be replaced by a quiet fury which he found strangely *attractive*.

'You think I'm someone you can just move around the place however it suits you, like a pawn on a chess board?' she demanded. 'You can't just rearrange my life for me and you certainly can't *buy* me. I'm not one of your adoring subjects, Corso—in fact, I'm the very opposite!'

Again Corso felt the frisson of unexpected heat, because he was finding her truculence intensely provocative. Her rosy lips were parted. Her cheeks were flushed pink. And despite the thick sweater and workmanlike trousers which flapped around her ankles, he was moved by an urgent desire to take her in his arms and kiss her.

'I would advise you to consider two things,' he said unevenly, as the blood pounded hot and sweet around his veins.

'Which are?'

Briefly, he savoured her challenge before preparing to quash it, because surely to reprimand her would remind her of the natural order of things. 'Firstly, I do not expect to be spoken to in such a manner.'

'Well, there's a simple solution to that. You can always leave.' She tilted her chin. 'Nobody's stopping you.'

'And secondly,' he continued, trying to ignore the thick plait swaying like a blonde snake against the luscious curve of her breasts. 'I think you'll find that interest rates on credit cards are very high. And if you're not careful, you could spend the rest of your life servicing your debt.'

He got a reaction then and it was more profound than he had expected. All the fight went out of her. Like a hot needle lancing into a balloon, she seemed instantly to deflate. As she slumped back onto the chair, her face grew even paler. Her grey eyes were filled with alarm and a look of fleeting reproach, which somehow made him feel guilty. But not for long.

'What are you talking about?' she husked.

'If you like, we could play games all evening, Rosie.' He shrugged. 'You could feign ignorance and outrage. Or you could accept that I know all about your current difficulties.'

'What...?' she whispered. 'What do you know?'

'I know about your large credit card debt. That the reason you're able to live in this cottage is because you help clean the big house of the estate on which it stands. I gather you have a wealthy absentee Sicilian owner to thank for that. And living rent-free enables most of your salary to reduce the money your mother owes to the courts, which is a frightening amount, by most people's standards. I know that you and your sister are guarantors and committed to paying it off.' He paused, and suddenly he was curious. 'What did she do, Rosie?'

He saw the faint flicker of fear which crossed her pale features. 'I'm surprised you haven't found that out, too.'

He shrugged. 'My investigation threw up only the bare facts, which were sufficient for my needs.' He narrowed his eyes as he looked at her. 'But I'm advising you that if radical action isn't taken quickly it could ruin your and Bianca's future, because long-term debt can grind you down.'

'And someone in your position would know all about long-term debt, of course,' she said sarcastically.

But Rosie's heart had started racing like one of the high-speed trains she rode every day of her working life. *How* had he found out their secret, when she and Bianca had done everything possible to keep the whole affair quiet?

And then she wondered how she could have been so naïve.

His advisors would have rooted around to discover stuff about her—just as they must have known exactly when she would arrive home today. They would have studied her shifts to ensure that the King didn't turn up to an empty cottage. He was simply using the knowledge which was always available to him.

'Are you…are you trying to *blackmail* me, Corso? Is that what this is all about?'

He laughed then, but she thought it sounded as empty as the cruel wind which sometimes howled in the trees outside her cottage, during the long months of winter.

'Don't be so melodramatic,' he remonstrated silkily. 'What would be the point of that? I am not in the business of destroying lives. I'm just pointing out that if you do me a favour, I could return the compliment and do one for you. It could be mutually beneficial, don't you think?'

Her head was spinning but, despite the magic wand temptation of having the Mediterranean king cancel the debt, Rosie knew she had to refuse—because warning signs were leaping up in front of her like road blocks. She didn't *need* his help. She and Bianca were managing on their own…just. She didn't *want* to make herself beholden to his immense privilege and power. She had weaned herself off Monterosso and its spurious glamour. She'd turned her back on her former life and put it in the past.

Plus, she didn't like him. Not any more. She found him proud and cold and arrogant. It didn't help that she had started wanting him in a way she'd never wanted anyone before. But the things you wanted and the things you got were two very different things.

'My answer is still no,' she said, ignoring the disbelief which made his autocratic features grow so cold. 'And now, I'm going to have to cut this visit short, I'm afraid. I need to do some cleaning over at the big house because Signor Corsini is flying a bunch of guests over from Palermo next weekend and he likes everything looking its best.'

But to her surprise Corso didn't react to the kind of dismissal he was unlikely to have experienced before. He just put his hand in the breast pocket of his leather jacket and pulled out a card, his expression still unyielding. It was the same stony countenance which was stamped on the front of every Monterossian coin and, for a moment, Rosie felt slightly intimidated.

But then he wrong-footed her and afterwards she wondered if it had been deliberate. He walked across the room towards her, covering the tiny space in seconds until he was standing directly in front of her—tall and golden, dominant and beautiful. A glowing god of man, pulsing with life and virility. Rosie gazed up at him as he took her hand, slipping the card into her palm before gently closing her fingers around it, and the resulting spark which fizzed over her skin was just…

Electric.

It was the briefest of touches yet her body rippled in instant response—as if she had spent her whole life waiting for him to touch her like that. Did he feel it too? Was that why he suddenly tensed, as if someone were about to land a blow on his solar plexus? Why he fixed her with that questioning golden gaze which seemed to burn right through her? She held her breath—almost as if she were waiting for him to do something else. Like what? Pull her into his arms and kiss her? Wasn't that what her fevered imagination was conjuring up?

But he didn't.

Of course he didn't.

His lips simply curved with a hint of mockery as he let go of her hand.

'Why don't you think about what I've said, Rosie? In my experience, it's always better to sleep on a proposition, before coming to a decision.'

His words hung in the air like silken baubles as, noiselessly, he let himself out of the cottage.

CHAPTER FIVE

'HE SAID *WHAT*?'

Rosie very nearly pulled a face but she didn't want to irritate her sister any more than she was already. She didn't want to repeat herself either, because she suspected that Bianca had registered every word she'd said and just wanted to mull them over.

That was the trouble with these video phone calls, she thought gloomily. You couldn't pretend. Your reaction was there for all to see—no matter how fuzzy the pixilation on the computer screen, or the fact that you were talking to someone in faraway Venice.

'I told you,' she said dully. 'Corso knows about Mum.'

'*What* does he know?'

'That she owes masses of money.'

'Does he know why?'

'It appears not, although that could just be an act. With Corso, you never know.'

'Tell me again what he said.'

Rosie swallowed. 'He wants to make full use of the Forrester name—to cash in on Dad's reputation and the fact that he discovered the jewels. He wants to exploit the fact that I'm Lionel's daughter and that I've got a degree in art history—well, I will have soon, hopefully. Which is presumably why he's offered me a ridiculous amount of money to go on a tour of the collection with him.'

'How much money?' asked her sister quickly.

As Rosie repeated the incredible sum, she was greeted with complete silence—which was rare. On screen she could see Bianca chewing her bottom lip, the way she used to do when she was at boarding school—studying harder than anyone else in her year. The dazzling star student Rosie had spent her life being unfavourably compared to.

'And you said, what?' Bianca demanded.

'What do you think I said? I refused, of course.' Rosie tried to iron out the defensiveness in her voice and to silence the thought which was telling her she was being unreasonable. 'I don't want to go anywhere with *him*,' she added fiercely. 'Especially not on a whistle-stop tour of three big cities I've never been to before.'

'Why not?'

Because suddenly I've started to fancy him. Because he makes me want to do things I've never done before and feel stuff I've never felt before. Because, because, because...

'He's insufferable!' she breathed. 'I'd forgotten just how arrogant he can be.'

Bianca gave her a look. 'Good heavens. How things change! I always thought the sky went dark whenever he sat down. It was always "Corso this" and "Corso that".' She huffed out a great big sigh. 'But that's all irrelevant.'

Rosie screwed up her face as she looked at the screen, because there was something in Bianca's tone which she recognised of old, and it was making foreboding creep over her skin. 'I'm not sure what you're talking about.'

'Then let me enlighten you, dear Rosie,' said Bianca—her studiedly patient tone morphing into the natural bossiness of a big sister. 'Corso's wealth can wipe out this debt for us—and that can't come a moment too soon. I'm fed up with scrimping and saving, just because of the stupid mistake our mother made. I don't want to be saddled with money worries for the rest of my life and neither should you. So here's what

you do. You ring him and tell him you'll agree
to do what he wants.' There was a dramatic
pause. 'Only you ask for twice as much money.'

If Rosie had been on a conventional phone
call, this would have been the moment when
she probably would have dropped the handset
and smashed it. 'Are you out of your mind?'
she breathed. 'I can't do that! What he's offer-
ing is more than generous!'

'Rubbish! It'll be like small change to him.
Think about it. Wouldn't it be nice to use the
extra to get Mum a decent place of her own,
near her sister, where she can lick her wounds
and find some kind of peace?' On screen, Bianca swept a glossy handful of black hair
away from her face. 'I don't see why Corso
Andrea da Vignola can't dig deeper into his
pockets—he is one of the richest men in the
world, after all.'

'I know he is.' Rosie swallowed, but her
throat still felt like sandpaper. 'But I don't feel
comfortable asking for more.'

'Why not?'

What could she possibly say? That she didn't
want Corso to think she was greedy and grasp-
ing? It didn't *matter* what he thought of her,
did it? Or maybe the truth was more insidious.
What would Bianca say if she admitted that her

major reservation was far more frightening? How would her worldly sister react if Rosie blurted out this stupid desire which seemed to have come out of nowhere? Which was that she wanted to melt into the King's powerful arms and offer her virginity to him, despite his arrogance and deep sense of entitlement?

Wouldn't that be enough of a let-out clause?

But she couldn't do that. For a start she would never admit that to anyone, not even her sister. And if she forced herself to discount Corso's physical impact, his offer made nothing but sense. Because Bianca was right. Sometimes Rosie felt as if the regular repayments were chipping away at her soul as well as her bank account. Why should *her* weakness around the Monterossian king prevent her from taking a step which would liberate them both?

She sighed. 'I suppose I'll have to do it.'

'Excellent.' Bianca flashed a cat-like smile. 'Keep me posted, little sister.' Suddenly there was a pinging noise and the screen went blank.

Rosie rose from the little desk which was shoved next to the wardrobe in the cottage's only bedroom. It was all very well to be bullish when she was talking to Bianca, but now she was filled with an overwhelming sense of dread at the thought of what lay ahead. She stared down at the discreetly expensive card he'd given her. It said simply: Corso of Monterosso, and next to his name was a phone number. All she had to do was to ring him.

But it took ages for her to pluck up the courage and, in the meantime, she procrastinated. She went over to the big house to check that everything was in place for Lucio Corsini's visit, before the temporary housekeeper, chef and butler arrived to cater for the tycoon's weekend party.

And that was another thing. Her cottage accommodation was provided free in return for keeping an eye on the property of the wealthy Sicilian. How would Lucio react when she told him she intended to be absent for a whole month while she waltzed off with the King of Monterosso?

Before she had time to change her mind, Rosie grabbed her phone and tapped out the number he'd given her, holding her breath as she prepared herself for the velvety onslaught of his voice. But instead of getting Corso, it went straight to one of his assistants, who introduced herself as Ivana.

'The King would like you to come in and see him in person.'

'But, I—'

'The embassy is in Belgrave Square,' continued Ivana, with the calm delivery of a woman who never deviated from her boss's wishes. 'I understand that you work in London, so it shouldn't be a problem. Just tell me what time suits and I'm sure we can work something into His Majesty's schedule. And please don't worry about transport. We can easily send a car to pick you up.'

'No, thank you,' said Rosie grimly. Imagining a royal car turning up at the Paddington train depot! What on earth would all her co-workers say if they saw the Monterossian flag fluttering on the bonnet? 'I'll make my own way.'

Which was how she found herself cycling through the drizzle to the quiet tree-lined streets of Belgravia the following afternoon. Past the imposing houses she rode before chaining her bike to a railing outside the beautiful, white-stuccoed building which housed the Monterossian embassy, where the two burly-looking men who guarded the entrance stared at her askance. But Rosie didn't care. So what if she was dripping rainwater onto their pristine marble floor, or was already getting hot and sweaty beneath her waterproof jacket? Corso had demanded to *see* her—so see her he would, warts and all.

Nevertheless, she felt sticky and crumpled as she was shown to the King's grand suite of offices on the first floor, past sleek women and equally sleek men who didn't lift their gazes from their computer screens. Over an endless expanse of pale wood she walked until at last she was shown into the inner sanctum of the monarch's office and, to her surprise, Corso was alone.

He sat behind a monster of a desk—ancient, carved blackwood by the look of it—and her attention was captured by a crystal paperweight which threw vivid rainbow light across the polished surface. Behind him were a couple of exquisite paintings of Monterosso—one depicting the silvery shimmer of the iconic lake which edged the country's capital and the other a landscape view of the wild mountain range which lay to the north of the country. She didn't want to feel a jab of nostalgia but there it was, all the same.

And when Rosie could distract her gaze no longer, she allowed it to fall on the flame-haired man who was leaning back in his chair, studying her with amusement quirking the edges of his lips, as if he was perfectly aware that she'd

been trying to look anywhere other than at him.
She couldn't deny that he looked delectable—
or that the roof of her mouth had dried with
instant desire, but hopefully she disguised her
reaction well enough with a small, forced smile.

At first glance, his dark suit, pale shirt and a
tie of amber silk made him seem the embodi-
ment of the contemporary man, but a portrait
of one of his ancestors on a nearby wall and the
identical glint in Corso's eyes reminded her of
his background. He was privileged. Ruthless
and powerful. He didn't care about her, or her
feelings. He just wanted what suited him.

*That was how royal dynasties managed to
survive.*

And to dominate.

'Rosie,' he purred, and she could hear the satisfaction in his voice. 'Why don't you remove
that dripping garment and come and sit down?'

She didn't want to sit down. She didn't want
to be here, but her skin was tingling as if she
were standing in front of a naked flame and so
she peeled off her sopping cagoule and hung it
on the back of the chair. Sinking into the sur-
prisingly comfortable seat on the other side of
the desk, she looked at him questioningly. 'I
gather you wanted to see me in person?'

'I did. And I will take your presence here as

acceptance.' His eyes narrowed. 'You will do as I ask?'

'Yes. I've spoken to my sister and she thinks...' She shrugged. 'We both think I should accept your offer.'

'Excellent.'

Rosie opened her lips to speak, but she was finding it harder to replicate Bianca's demand than she'd imagined. 'But on one condition.'

'On one condition,' he repeated, only now his voice had taken on an edge of something she didn't recognise. 'And what might that be, I wonder?'

'I want more,' she blurted out into the awkward silence which followed his question.

He raised his eyebrows. 'More?' he echoed unhelpfully.

'Money.' She tried not to flinch as she saw contempt hardening his features. 'I... I want more money.'

Corso felt a slow rush of anger invading his blood—but the feeling was underpinned with something else. Something he hadn't expected, nor wanted to feel—and that was a deep sense of disappointment. Because yes, he had pushed hard to get Rosie Forrester to agree to his offer—but he had justified his behaviour with the knowledge that, ultimately, his generosity would benefit her family. She was her father's daughter after all, and part of him had hoped Lionel's liberal attitude might have percolated down to his younger daughter. Had he imagined that she might regard him as a person, rather than just a symbol of power and wealth? That, having had time to think about the many benefits his offer would bring, she might also wish to accompany him for old times' sake, and even be grateful for his intervention? Yes. Stupidly enough, he had.

Silently, he cursed his foolish idealism, focussing on her true nature as a way of sidelining the sudden stab to his heart. Why, she was as avaricious as any other woman he'd ever met! And perhaps not quite as clever as she imagined. Wasn't she aware that her attitude would destroy any lingering traces of affection he'd held for her? Yet in many ways it was easier to be angry with her than to desire her. And definitely easier to concentrate on her blatant greed, rather than the brother who awaited him in New York.

The brother whose very existence is a testament to the sham of your parents' supposedly perfect marriage.

'How much do you want?' he demanded harshly, but at this she blushed and the brief flicker of hurt which clouded her grey eyes was confusing. He shook his head in frustration. She ought to make up her mind about the part she was trying to play. About whether she wanted to come over as acquisitive or sensitive. About who she really was.

'Er, I haven't quite worked it out yet,' she prevaricated.

'Which is just about the most hopeless piece of negotiation I've witnessed in a long time,' he snapped. 'What exactly do you want the money for, Rosie?'

She moved a little awkwardly, which had the unfortunate effect of making his gaze want to stray to the luscious swell of her breasts, which managed to transform a perfectly ordinary sweater into one of the most provocative pieces of clothing he'd ever seen. But, with a huge effort of will, he kept his eyes fixed firmly on her face.

'I'd rather not say.'

'Tough, because I'd rather you would. I might even make it a condition.' He flicked her a disdainful look. 'Or maybe you think you have the monopoly on conditions, Rosie?'

For a moment she seemed about to object, but maybe she realised she was on shaky ground because she chewed her bottom lip, before nodding in silent assent.

'It's to pay off the debts and buy Mum a house,' she said at last. 'Once the court judgement against her has been settled. She's renting a cheap bedsit in the middle of London at the moment and we'd like her to have a little cottage in the country, near to where her sister lives.'

Corso leaned back in his chair, her selfless declaration taking him by surprise, reluctantly forcing him to reassess his jaundiced view of her. Because he didn't want to think of her as thoughtful, or caring. In fact, he didn't want to think about her at all. 'Don't you think it's time you told me how she got herself into so much debt?' he probed. 'Since you're expecting me to bankroll her future.'

Rosie wanted to tell him it was none of his business, but she could see that maybe it was. In a way, she had *made* it his business, by asking him to increase his offer. And if she didn't tell him, he would find out soon enough—if he were so inclined. So why not give him her version—even if there wasn't really a way of conveying the facts which didn't make her mother look a little sad?

She hoped her shrug hid the pain—because

that was the trouble with remembering. It hurt. 'My mother was never the same after Dad died.'

'They were that rare thing,' he observed. 'A married couple who seemed genuinely to care for one another.'

She wondered if she had imagined the bitterness in his voice—but it wasn't exactly the sort of thing she could ask him about, was it? 'Yes, they did. They cared for each other very deeply. That's probably why she missed him so badly after he died. She felt lost without him. She went to pieces and never seemed to put herself back together again. Way too soon after his death she went onto an online dating site to try to find herself a new partner—desperately looking to replace what she had with Dad.' She hesitated. 'So that, unfortunately, the predictable happened.'

He narrowed his eyes. 'The predictable being, what?'

She wanted to tell him to use his imagination, but what was the point? She didn't think Corso would have a clue what she was talking about. He didn't operate in the same kind of world she lived in and she doubted whether he even *had* an imagination. 'She lost her heart to a man she'd never even met. How insane is that?'

'*Losing* your heart to anyone is something I've never understood,' he said, his voice edged with acid. 'But yes, that kind of behaviour is particularly insane.' He leaned back in the sumptuous leather chair, the spring sunshine streaming in from the tall windows and setting the thick mane of his hair on fire. 'So what happened?'

'She gave him money every time he came up with yet another excuse about why he wasn't able to meet her in person.' Rosie gave a hollow laugh as the long-repressed words rushed from her mouth and she realised she'd never talked about it with anyone else, other than her sister. She had hidden it away, like a dirty little secret. 'It was the usual story. He was expecting a bank transfer which had been held up. He was due a huge inheritance any day. An ex-partner owed him hundreds of thousands of pounds. To an outsider it would have sounded exactly what it was—a blatant lie and a scam. But whatever he told her, she believed him. She was putty in his hands—blinded by longing and influenced by the three most manipulative words in the English language.'

'Those words being?'

'Oh, come on.' She met the question in his eyes. 'Do you really not know *that*, Corso?'

He lifted his shoulders expressively. 'I love you?'

And the craziest thing of all was that Rosie started wondering what it would be like if the flame-haired King were actually making that statement to her and that he *meant* it—rather than as a scornful query. She shuddered. What was the *matter* with her? Was she in danger of behaving as foolishly as her mother?

'You've got it in one,' she answered flippantly. 'By the time Bianca and I found out, it was too late. She'd lost everything—and more.' It had made her think a lot about grief. About loneliness. And for a while it had made her think that maybe she was lucky to have escaped all that. That maybe relationships weren't everything they were cracked up to be, if you could hurt so badly once they ended.

She looked at Corso and perhaps she was hoping for a smidgeon of understanding or empathy in his eyes, but she could read nothing in that hard, metallic gaze.

'Then perhaps we should acknowledge that my intervention is timely,' was all he said. 'And think about where we're headed, going forward.'

Rosie sat up very straight. 'Does that mean you agree to my price?'

'You might want to think carefully about

how you express yourself,' he advised caustically. 'Unless your intention is to make yourself sound like a commodity in the marketplace, being offered to the highest bidder.'

Corso heard her shocked intake of breath and, though something was urging him to go gently on her, he did not heed it. She was not the Rosie he remembered. She had become someone he didn't know. She looked different. She sounded different. 'Yes, I agree to your price,' he continued coldly. 'And because of that you will agree to my terms.'

A soft knock on the door interrupted him in mid-flow and, with a flicker of irritation, Corso looked up to see his assistant standing in the doorway. 'Yes, Ivana—what is it?'

'I have the Maraban ambassador on the line.'

He waved an impatient hand through the air. 'Give me five minutes.' As the door closed behind his assistant, he returned his gaze to Rosie. 'You will meet me in Paris in exactly one week's time.'

'No way. I can't just walk out of my job that quickly,' she protested.

'This is the deal. Take it or leave it. It's not up for negotiation. We are showing the collection in three major cities—Paris, New York and London—and I want you there from the start.

One of my assistants can liaise directly with your employers about temporarily replacing you, if that makes it simpler.'

'You think I am so easily replaceable?'

'Everyone is replaceable,' he said wryly. 'Even kings.'

'Even you, Corso? Surely not!'

Corso was tempted to tell her not to talk to him like that. He didn't want fire and feistiness, or teasing. He wanted her to be greedy and calculating. He wanted her to help reinforce his prejudices about women, which were deeply engrained—especially now. He didn't need her words to remind him of a different time, when life had seemed so simple. When he had been able to regard her as something close to a friend.

But it wasn't friendship he was feeling now. It was lust, pure and simple.

His gaze travelled over her. Her sweater was plain, her jeans faded—but the cheap clothes failed to conceal the fact that her body was strong and healthy. Or that her firm curves had obviously been acquired through hard work and natural exercise—not from narcissistic hours spent gazing at her own reflection in the mirror of a gym. Her thick hair was as pale as the dawn and the soft dimple in her cheek oddly compelling. But that kind of thinking was deeply unhelpful. *He needed to concentrate on her inadequacies, not on the way she was inexplicably turning him on.*

'We also need to find you some new clothes,' he said abruptly.

'You're assuming I have nothing appropriate of my own?'

'I really have no idea,' he drawled. 'Do you?'

Rosie glowered. Of course she didn't have anything suitable for an international royal trip. Her railway uniform and the casual clothes she favoured when she wasn't working would hardly go down a storm. Why, she only owned one dress and she couldn't remember the last time she'd worn it.

'Sorry, I'm fresh out of diamonds and lace!'

'You won't need those for TV. Simple works best for television.'

'Television?' she echoed, sitting bolt upright. 'Are you out of your mind?'

'Careful, Rosie—my aides might not take kindly to you casting doubts on my sanity.'

'Corso.' She cleared her throat. 'Listen.'

'I'm listening.'

'I can't possibly go on TV. I don't have any experience.'

'You've got the only experience anyone ever

needs. You know your subject, don't you? You know all about your father...' There was a faint crack in his voice, before he recovered his velvety delivery. 'And all the treasures he unearthed,' he concluded.

'It isn't as simple as that. How can I possibly go on television? Me, of all people! I'm not a media personality—I'm a railway worker. I serve cups of tea and sandwiches on the train.'

'Don't worry. These days everybody gets their ten minutes of fame. We'll make sure you get a crash course in media training before we throw you to the lions.'

'Corso—'

'Rosie, I really don't have time for this.' He gave an impatient click of his fingers. 'If I feed your fear, it will only grow. I'll see you in Paris. My office will be in touch about the arrangements.'

He was staring at her pointedly and Rosie realised that the door had silently opened and Ivana was standing on the threshold, waiting to escort her from the premises, like a gatecrasher at a party. Her face hot, she rose to her feet, picking up her helmet and dripping cagoule. Her hand was shaking, she realised—and not just because Corso had ended the conversation so abruptly. Nor even because he'd high-handedly announced that he was going to provide her with a brand-new wardrobe. No, it was nothing to do with that. It was all to do with *him*. With his gleaming eyes and flame-kissed hair and a hard body which no amount of fancy clothes could disguise. How dared he make her want him like this?

Outside, she unchained her bicycle and stared up at the enormous first-floor windows of his offices, in time to see a silhouetted figure appear. It was too shadowy to be able to make out his features with any degree of clarity, but the hard-bodied frame was unmistakably that of the King as he stared down at her. She waited for him to lift his hand in a wave of acknowledgement—but no such sign came and she felt an undeniable twist of disappointment as he turned away from the window, as if dismissing her.

Rosie's heart raced as she wheeled her bike away. Didn't he realise how difficult it would be for someone like her to go on television, wearing stuff somebody else had chosen? Maybe that was the kind of magnanimous gesture which would thrill a certain kind of woman—but that woman wasn't her. She wasn't going to act like some grateful Cinderella, if that was what he was expecting. She would accept what she was given in a very grown-up way and afterwards she would hand everything back—borrowed clothes for a borrowed life. She would conduct herself appropriately because she knew how—she'd watched how royal circles operated often enough. And she would work her socks off, because she'd never been afraid of hard work.

Somehow—she wasn't sure how—she would overcome her fears and be an asset to Monterosso and its people. She would bring pride to the Forrester name. All she needed to do was to focus on the big prize which awaited her, which would liberate her and Bianca from the constant worry of debt and give their mother the type of home they thought she'd lost for ever.

Most important of all, she would keep her desire for Corso hidden.

Actually, she was going to do more than that. She would trample it ruthlessly underfoot, until it was nothing but a dusty memory of her own stupidity.

Somehow that seemed like the biggest ask of all.

CHAPTER SIX

THE TELEVISION STUDIO was buzzing with activity
and people were running around in every direction. Impossibly glamorous people in ripped
jeans, jabbering in French and gesturing excit-
edly with their hands. Rosie felt another stab of
apprehension as she glanced around.

'Is it always like this?' she asked nervously,
twisting her fingers together and wishing the
palms of her hands weren't quite so sweaty.

The producer—who looked about twelve
but was probably about the same age as her—
shook his head. 'It is because we have a king
here,' he said, giving a conspiratorial grin as
he thumped his fist against his chest in a crude
attempt to mimic a rapidly beating heart. 'All
the women—they want him to notice them. I
think that they want to be his queen—despite
the fact that we are a proud republic!'

Rosie looked up at the monitor, where Corso's sculpted features dominated the screen, beneath which a small crowd of women were standing, watching him avidly. His skin glowed like old gold, his metallic eyes lashed with ebony and his dark hair lit with fire. She could see exactly why they were watching him because he really *did* look like an old-fashioned matinee idol as he conducted the interview— but all she could think about was the ordeal which lay ahead. She was up next for her interview in front of the camera and already she was frozen with fear. Despite the make-up artist dabbing her brow every other second, it remained hot and clammy and her heart was pounding like mad beneath the horrible black dress they'd given her to wear.

Half sick with dread, she turned away from the monitor and walked carefully to the far end of the studio, desperate to be alone. For a moment she stood there in blissful solitude, drawing in ragged gulps of air as she tried to calm herself, though it did little to quell her spiralling fears. How could all those articles on deep breathing be so wrong, and how on earth had she ended up *here*—in a Parisian television studio, waiting for one of France's most respected art historians to quiz her about the ancient jewels of Monterosso?

She couldn't do it.

She *wouldn't* do it.

Already events had taken on the surreal air of a twisted fairy tale—but instead of a travelling in a souped-up pumpkin, she had been plucked from her cottage in the forest before being whisked by limousine to London, then flown to Paris on the King's private jet. From the airstrip she had been taken to the Monterossian embassy on the fancy Rue du Faubourg Saint-Honoré to a suite of almost unimaginable splendour. She'd scarcely had time to brush her teeth before a scarily sophisticated stylist had turned up with a bunch of clothes for her to try on, which were the last thing Rosie would ever have chosen to wear herself. Silk, chiffon and leather were very definitely *not* her thing and she'd nearly passed out when she'd spotted a couple of the price tags.

Even worse was the accompanying lingerie because surely underwear was supposed to cover you up—rather than revealing more of her body than she was comfortable with. She had tried to refuse them, but, once again, had been overruled. It seemed that the palace was controlling everything—or rather, Corso was. He seemed to have been orchestrating things from a distance—and it was all too much. She felt like a puppet having its strings tweaked by an unseen master, which should have made her deeply indignant. So why did a scary shiver of excitement skate its way down her spine, every time she thought about it?

'Rosie? Ah. It *is* you. Once again, I find you hiding in the shadows. This is getting to be a habit. Is it a deliberate ploy, I wonder? An attempt to force people to seek you out?'

Rosie tensed as Corso's sardonic question rippled through the air like a brush of velvet and she turned to face him, resenting the sudden rush of awareness which sizzled through her as he walked across the studio floor to join her. She had convinced herself she was going to feel nothing but detachment when she saw him again, but her conviction was fast disappearing—melted away by the powerful heat of his presence. No man had a right to be this gorgeous, she thought despairingly. On the small screen he had been captivating—but up close he was positively *distracting*.

His dark designer suit hugged the contours of his muscular frame and he'd left the top two buttons of his silk shirt open, making him appear far more relaxed than usual. It was the first time she had spoken to him since arriving in France, because he'd been meeting with politicians and CEOs or so closely surrounded by his security people that nobody could get near him. She'd tried telling herself it was a bonus not to have to endure his company, or to have to gaze into the mocking distraction of his metallic gaze. The only trouble with that statement was that it wasn't true.

'I came over here because I wanted a little time on my own before my interview,' she said pointedly.

But he refused to take the hint. 'Are you ready?' he questioned, jabbing a finger against the face of his watch. 'They'll be calling you in a minute.'

'No,' she mumbled, his effect on her forgotten as her throat grew dry with renewed panic at the thought of what she had to do. 'If you want the truth, I'm nowhere near ready. If I could, I'd walk out of here right now. Get the earliest flight back to London and go back to my old life.'

She expected him to snub or berate her, or tell her to pull herself together, but maybe she had misjudged him. Because beneath the subdued light of the studio, the King's eyes narrowed thoughtfully.

'What's the matter, Rosie?' he questioned softly.

She wished he wouldn't use that tone with

her because it reminded her of the past, when he'd been kind to her. It made her feel vulnerable—and that was the last way she could afford to feel right now. 'Is that a serious question?' she demanded. 'You mean, apart from the fact that I'm trussed up in this dull dress which makes me look so frumpy? Or that these shoes are so high that I can barely walk in them without risking a fracture?'

Corso frowned, because her self-assessment was so off the mark, it was almost laughable. When he'd walked into the studio today, he hadn't recognised her. The inevitable ripple of excitement followed by total silence must have alerted her to the fact that the royal party had arrived, but Rosie's back had remained turned to him, for she had been engrossed in reading something. Yet for once he had been prepared to overlook the huge breach of protocol. He remembered his gaze homing in on her, as if something outside his control were compelling him to do so—and that was unusual. Her black dress was deceptively simple, yet somehow it managed to emphasise her incredibly curvy shape, which reminded him of an old-fashioned movie star. Just as the high-heeled black shoes showcased a pair of beautifully toned legs, which gleamed beneath the studio lights. Her hair was caught back in an elegant chignon and, as he'd registered the few strands of palest blonde which had tumbled onto the slim column of her neck, he was hit by a powerful thunderbolt of something he didn't recognise.

Because this really was Rosie.

A remarkably different Rosie from one he'd ever seen before.

And one who was completely out of her depth, he realised, with an unusual degree of insight.

'You look sensational,' he said slowly.

'No, I don't.'

Corso wondered what made him seek to reassure her further. The knowledge that a flurry of nerves had the potential to ruin her interview and garner adverse publicity for his tour? Possibly. Or maybe it was more fundamental than that. Because the truth was that he hadn't been able to stop thinking about her and he couldn't work out why. She'd been invading his thoughts at the most inappropriate moments. Those cushion-soft lips and cloud-grey eyes. Her defiance. Her compliance. Different sides of a woman who was fascinating him more than she should.

And yet her physical transformation from

duckling to swan had only managed to highlight her inherent freshness and lack of guile—
and since these were qualities he rarely came
across in his daily life, shouldn't he help pre-
serve them?

'Believe me when I tell you that you do. You
look amazing,' he contradicted. 'And that per-
petrating a negative attitude about yourself is
a waste of time.'

'It's easy for you to talk.'

'And just as easy for you to listen,' he ad-
monished sternly.

'You were the one who told me I needed to
change my image,' she mumbled. 'How is that
going to do anything for my confidence?'

'Surely you're able to take a little construc-
tive advice,' he came back coolly. 'You've got
to start believing in yourself, Rosie. As of now.
The camera has the power to pick up every
single one of your insecurities and magnify
them—and that won't do you any favours.'

'If that's supposed to be encouraging, I'd hate
to hear you being negative,' she said moodily.

Corso had almost forgotten what it was like
for someone to speak to him as an equal—
even though she would never be his *real* equal.
Nonetheless, her words provoked an unexpected flicker of a smile as he fixed his gaze

on the high-heeled black shoes which made her legs look so deliciously long. 'If you really can't walk in those,' he added, 'then I can offer my arm to support you.'

'I'm twenty-five, not a hundred and five! I don't think I've quite reached the stage of needing to use you as a crutch, Corso—though obviously I'm extremely grateful for the offer.'

But she smiled and it was the first time he had seen a genuine smile from her in a long time. It split through the intervening years like a knife ripping through a closed curtain, taking him by surprise. As did the sudden punch of his heart and the rush of something shockingly potent which was making his blood grow heated. Something he recognised with confusion and annoyance—because he'd never wanted her that way in the past.

I don't want to desire her, he told himself angrily.

I don't want to desire anyone, until the time is right.

His focus must be on finding his brother. *Not on how much he would like to spread open Rosie Forrester's soft thighs and put his head between them and lick her until she was crying out his name.*

With an effort, he adopted the mask of indifference which usually came so easily to him and flicked another glance at his watch. 'They're calling you. Just go in there and give it everything you've got. I'll wait for you in the car out front.'

She blinked at him. 'You'll wait for me?' she verified slowly. 'But the King waits for nobody.'

'Don't labour the point, Rosie,' he drawled. 'We can share a car back to the embassy. It makes perfect sense. If we save on fuel, it's so much better for the planet.'

His lazy words were so unexpected that Rosie giggled and she saw people turning to look at them, as if startled by the sound. Come to think of it, she was pretty startled herself—given her current state of nerves. She watched hungry female eyes following Corso as he swept from the studio and, as his entourage moved quickly to surround him, she warned herself never to join their adoring ranks. She mustn't start thinking he was funny, or sexy, or clever.

But maybe his words had been more comforting than she'd realised because her panic seemed to have evaporated as she sat down to face the interviewer. It helped that the niche arts programme had relatively modest audience figures and that the questioner knew loads about her dad. Which meant she was able to speak with genuine passion about the exquisite pearls and beaten gold jewellery which he'd discovered all those years ago. She spoke for longer than she'd anticipated and felt almost high with relief when finally she exited the studio. She felt more confident now in the skyscraper heels, and the heady atmosphere of springtime Paris helped lift her mood even further.

The TV studios were situated eight kilometres outside the city centre and she could hear birds singing amid the dark pink blooms of the horse-chestnut trees which lined the street. Bathed in bright sunshine, she looked around without much expectation, doubtful Corso would have hung around for this long and deciding that maybe she should walk for a while before taking the Metro back to the embassy. But no, there was the dark-windowed royal limousine parked by the edge of the pavement, the turquoise and purple of the Monterossian flag fluttering proudly on the gleaming black bonnet.

A member of the King's security detail stepped forward to open the door for her and Rosie slid inside, the fitted dress making her movements unusually cautious and slow. The door clicked shut to enclose her and her heart began to hammer as her eyes became accustomed to the dim light and she became aware of Corso's shadowed presence on the seat beside her, writing something by hand in a notebook.

He'd told her he would be here—so it was no big surprise—yet his impact on her was shockingly visceral. Suddenly she was glad she was sitting down. His muscular body was so powerful. His shoulders were so broad. Even the fingers which held his pen were gorgeous. What would it be like if those long fingers were stroking their way over her skin—lightly grazing her burning flesh? Her throat dried as his gaze washed over her and, to her horror, she realised she had started to tremble. Was it that which made her blurt out the first stupid thing which came into her head?

'You waited.'

He raised his eyebrows. 'I said I would.'

'I know, but...'

'But what, Rosie?' She heard the faint edge of exasperation in his voice. 'You don't consider me to be a man of my word?'

Rosie realised she had no idea what kind of man he was because most of the things she knew about Corso were things she'd read or heard from other people, and everyone knew that hearsay was unreliable. Yet she remembered the younger version very well. The Crown Prince whose mother had died. Who had hidden all his pain and grief behind an impenetrable mask, because that blanketing of emotion had been demanded of him—by his father, and by his royal destiny. Had that been the moment when the first layers of cynicism had started building around him, separating him from other people, or was that just inevitable when you inherited a throne and people always wanted something from you?

'Actually, I *do* believe you're a man of your word,' she said, the words more fervent than she had intended.

Corso was silent as he studied the gleam of her lips, for he was unused to receiving such heartfelt praise. Yet he had sought her good opinion of him, hadn't he? Now he found himself wondering why—and why he had dismissed his bemused aides to sit waiting in his limousine while Rosie Forrester finished her interview, he who had never waited for a woman in his life.

He knew why. It was obvious from the tension which was thrumming in the air between them, so powerful that he felt he could have reached out and touched it.

Desire.

Inexplicable, intense and unpredictable.

He might have successfully kept his sexual hunger at bay for the last seven years—but that didn't mean he didn't recognise it when it came along to hit him with the force of a sledgehammer. He stared unseeingly out of the window as the limousine began to move through the traffic, his thoughts coming thick and fast. Inheriting the throne had been a double-edged sword. First had come his realisation of the damage done to his country by his father's greed—and later still, the discovery of his duplicity and its grim legacy. Sickened by the revelations and determined to repair the destruction the late King had wrought, Corso had decided to wholeheartedly embrace celibacy, like the knights of old. Because women were a distraction and extra demands on his time were something he didn't need.

He had banished desire from his life through sheer effort of will and a determination not to be sucked in by its sweet promise. Employing a masochistic element of self-control, he had allowed himself a brief sense of satisfaction at successfully banishing the carnal needs of his body. It was as though he had acquired a special immunity against sexual hunger. But that hunger was washing over him now and it was taking him prisoner. Unremitting and un-relenting—it flooded through his veins like a rich rush of honey. It felt unbearably sweet to be alone in the back seat of a car with Rosie Forrester and he wondered if it was curiosity which had made him take this potentially risky step, or just his body's yearning to feel prop-erly alive again.

He observed her stiff posture as she sat be-side him. The way she kept crossing and un-crossing her legs, before resting her hands on her knees. She was probably trying to blot up the stickiness of her palms, but all she was doing was drawing his attention to her luscious thighs. And even though they were demurely covered in black linen, he couldn't stop think-ing about the soft flesh beneath and how much he would like to press his fingers against it.

His mind played a speeded-up version of what could happen next, if he pulled her into his arms and began to kiss her. It would be so easy. He gave a grim smile. It always was. The atmosphere between them was so electric that he imagined little would be required in the way of foreplay. Sometimes hot and urgent was best for the first time, he mused.

But *he wasn't going to have sex with her*

and not just because of his determination to remain celibate. Because this was Rosie he was thinking about. *Rosie.* The tomboy he'd once rescued from a tree. Who he'd taught how to tie knots. Who had been kind to him at a time when nobody else had known how to behave around him. What right did he have to contemplate intimacy with her and then inevitably break her heart?

So focus on something else, he told himself fiercely. Focus on the only reason she's here today—as the star turn for Monterossian PR and nothing more. Leaning back, he spoke from lips which were suddenly bone-dry. 'You did very well in there just now.'

'How do you know that, if you were waiting in the car?'

'My aides usually relay initial feedback from the interview, but in this instance...' He leaned forward to tap the blank screen of a TV fixed to the screen separating them from the driver. 'I watched you live.'

'You watched me live,' she repeated, before turning those grey eyes on him, and Corso felt as if he could have fallen straight into them, like diving into a silvery lake. 'Honestly?'

'Honestly,' he echoed gravely.

'And?'

'You were excellent. Much better than I had anticipated. As seasoned as a pro, in fact. Lionel would have been very proud.'

She bit her lip. 'That means a lot. I can't tell you how much.'

He wanted to tell her not to look at him like that—so wide-eyed and grateful that it was threatening to burrow beneath his defences. Nor to draw his attention to the succulence of her lips, which made him badly want to kiss them. He felt his fingers uncurl so that the pen he was holding slid to the floor of the car and only the clattering noise it made broke the fraught silence, alerting him to the fact that he had dropped it. Pleased by the distraction, Corso bent to pick it up himself but so, too, did Rosie. As they bent down to retrieve it, they reached towards the gleaming object at exactly the same time, their fingertips touching and briefly lingering. It was the faintest and most innocent of contacts and yet it was like…

Corso felt the pounding of his heart.

It was like a bolt of lightning forking through his body. It was making him grow hard. Making him want to pull her into his arms and pull the clips from her silky hair and then lay her down on that wide seat, and kiss her.

Her face was so close but he made no attempt to move his head away, even as his fingers closed around the pen before she could reach it. He could feel her warm breath on his skin and smell her scent—something subtle yet earthy, like sandalwood. The crackle of attraction between them was so strong he could almost hear it. And something stabbed at his heart as well as his gut as she looked at him with those wide grey eyes. As if he were the only man she had ever looked at like that.

Her lips were crying out for the press of his. The hard peaking of her nipples demanding he touch them. Temptation rippled over his skin and the urge to kiss her was overwhelming. But he would not give into temptation. He would not become a victim of desire. If this was a test of his own inner strength, he would pass it.

And wasn't denial good for the soul—if such a thing existed?

Abruptly, he sat up, distancing himself physically as well as emotionally—and emotional withdrawal was something he excelled at. Putting the pen away, he opened his notebook to study it—as if he were able to make sense of the indecipherable blur of his own handwriting—before glancing up to offer her a bland smile. His official smile. The one which reminded people never to get too close. 'Haven't you got a cell phone or something to play with, Rosie?' he murmured. 'Now that I've massaged your ego by complimenting you on your performance, I have some things which really need my attention.'

Even the most dense of people would have recognised his words as a dismissal, and Rosie Forrester was not dense. He saw the flicker of consternation which crossed her features and the way she chewed on her lip, as if distressed. Why was she looking so damned kittenish all of a sudden? he wondered angrily. Was she hoping for all the things he'd just been fantasising about?

But her thoughts were irrelevant.

All she needed to be aware of was that nothing was going to happen between them.

Nothing.

CHAPTER SEVEN

'I'm waiting for my guided tour, Rosie.'

A pair of dark brows were raised in arrogant query and Rosie's smile was nervous as Corso stood in front of her, looking mouth-wateringly delectable in his dark designer suit. With a minimum of fanfare, he'd arrived at the Musée des Antiquités moments before and been escorted straight into the exhibition room where she'd been working with Phillipe le Clerc, the museum's curator, for most of the day.

She tried to steady her suddenly ragged breathing, but it wasn't easy. None of this was easy. It was the first time she'd seen him since he'd driven her back from the TV studios yesterday afternoon, when for a moment the sexual tension between them had been so heightened that she'd thought he was about to kiss her.

Corso?

Kiss her?

Her?

How sad was that? As if Corso—having the pick of any woman he wanted—would choose to get intimate with her. Deciding she needed to put as much space as possible between them for the sake of her own sanity, she had slunk upstairs when they'd arrived back at the embassy. Then she had busied herself preparing for the upcoming exhibition, before picking at the meal she'd asked to be delivered to her room—a request which seemed to perplex the French maid who had delivered it. As if nobody in their right mind would choose to eat their dinner off a tray.

But she couldn't hide away from Corso for ever—especially not when he was towering above her beneath the bright lights of the museum, a faintly impatient look glinting from between his narrowed eyes as he demanded her attention. Bobbing a small curtsey in an attempt to highlight their difference in status, she produced her most efficient smile. 'I'm sure Monsieur le Clerc is far more qualified to show you around than I am,' she said. 'He is, after all, one of the greatest experts on ancient Mediterranean jewellery in all of Europe.'

'But it is you I want,' emphasised Corso—his silky command enough to make Phillipe melt away into the background, with a very Gallic shrug.

The King's words were distracting—his presence even more so. Suddenly Rosie felt as if she were alone with him again. As if they were the only two people in the world—even though the usual phalanx of guards were standing a respectful distance away. But that was the undeniable power of the man. He had the ability to make everyone else seem like shadows around him. And that was nothing new. She had always recognised that quality in him. What had changed was *her*—and the effect he was having on her. Despite her having elected to wear the most sensible components of her wardrobe, her body was reacting in ways she couldn't seem to control. Beneath the sawn-off linen trousers and silk shirt, her skin felt sensitised and prickly. Her breasts seemed to have acquired a new and alarming life of their own—their tips pressing uncomfortably against her new bra—and there was that distracting curl of heat again, low in her belly.

She needed to get a grip of herself before she did something stupid. She was supposed to be doing a job of work for him, that was all.

That was all.

'Very well,' she said crisply. 'Let me show

you around. We've made some changes to the order of the display cases.'

Indicating he should follow her, Rosie started at the first glass-covered case, beneath which were a set of small bracelets, intricately inlaid with amethyst, turquoise and lapis lazuli. 'We've decided to show the pieces chronologically,' she explained. 'And since the collection isn't very big we were able to contain it all within this one space, which makes it very accessible for the public. Look. These are the bracelets which were made for Queen Aurelia when she was just a baby—though it's doubtful if she ever wore them. See how tiny they are.'

But her professionalism dissolved the moment Corso stepped closer to study the contents of the display case and Rosie felt a terrifying desire to reach out and touch him. To run her fingertips over the shaded jut of his jaw to see how rough it felt.

She cleared her throat as they made their way towards the next exhibit. 'As we move through the room,' she said quickly, 'we can see the magnitude and size of her jewellery collection increasing—culminating in the precious suite she was given on her marriage and then on the birth of her first child.' She paused. 'But we saved the best for last, which isn't jewellery at all. Because here we have the only known statue of the young Queen—probably carved during the first year of her marriage. It's...it's beautiful, isn't it? So incredibly clear, and detailed. It's almost as if she's here with us.'

Corso inclined his head, admiring her fluency and knowledge and noticing the way her face came to life when she spoke about the ancient artefacts—her features filled with fire and passion.

With an effort, he dragged his attention back to the statue. He had seen it before—many times, for it had been languishing in airtight storage in Monterosso for years—but here it seemed to assume a special poignancy when assembled with the burial jewels. It seemed to emphasise the terrible awareness of hindsight, knowing the shadow of death was already hovering over the young Queen. He wondered, if he were to die now, what his lasting legacy would be and whether the brother he was seeking would choose to inherit the heavy mantle of the throne. Had he made Monterosso as good as he possibly could? Wiping out some of the damage done to it in the past? Had he done the best he could?

Suddenly he thought about his mother, unprepared for the shaft of pain which clenched at his heart. His recent discovery of an illegitimate brother made an already complicated relationship with his past even more so—and usually, he controlled access to his memories with steely rigidity. But not so now. Was it Rosie's familiarity, or the strangely informal relationship he'd once shared with her, which made him want to confide in her the secrets he carried with him, despite knowing how misguided such a confidence would be?

Attempting to quash the muddle of his thoughts, he asked a question to which he already knew the answer. 'How old would the Queen have been when this was modelled?'

'Twenty-five.'

'The same age as you,' he observed.

'Well, yes.'

He heard her miss a beat—as if she was surprised he'd remembered, or that he had deigned to mention it. 'And by then she had already given birth to one child and was pregnant with the second,' he continued.

'That's right.'

There was a pause and afterwards he found himself wondering what made him ask a question which had no relevance at all. 'Haven't you ever wanted to marry and have a family of your own, Rosie?'

He saw her face working awkwardly, as if he had put her on the spot.

'I'm not a big fan of the institution,' she said, at last. 'I've seen very few examples which make me want to rush to join in.'

'Not even your own parents?'

She shrugged. 'You can never be objective about your parents' marriage, can you? Anyway, you make marriage sound like a choice. Like something you can just decide to do—like picking a can of beans off the supermarket shelf.'

'I guess, for me, it is a bit like that.'

'Because you're a man?'

'Because I'm a king.'

'How easy you make it sound, Corso. Like clockwork! Any idea when this auspicious event might take place, so that I can buy myself a hat?'

'You might not be invited to the wedding.'

'Well, tell me anyway—so at least I can start saving up for a toaster!'

He failed to hold back the glimmer of a smile. 'There is no definite time-frame, but it is going to happen,' he said resolutely. 'When I am satisfied that my country is finally on the right track for a prosperous future, then it will be time to take a bride.'

'And where are you planning to take her?' she asked.

He ignored the flippant interruption, finding himself in full flow as he answered a question nobody had ever dared ask before. His courtiers wouldn't dream of being so presumptuous and he had spurned close relationships for so long that keeping his own counsel had become second nature. 'She must be of royal blood, of course,' he continued thoughtfully. 'That is a given to a man in my position. I have always found it ironic that, although an eligible king can have his pick of almost any woman he desires, his choice of whom he can marry is, by necessity, limited.'

'I can't believe you're saying all this,' she breathed.

'I'm saying it because it's the truth,' he retorted. 'Even if it isn't a particularly fashionable one.'

'And does the lucky, high-born woman have any say in your decision to marry her, or is her fate sealed like a sacrificial lamb?'

'You don't think most woman would be delighted to marry me, Rosie?'

Rosie could hear the mockery in his voice but also the unmistakable arrogance. And the most annoying thing was that he probably *was* speaking the truth because she could imagine there were plenty of women who would want to marry him. He was, after all, a golden-eyed sex god who ruled one of the most powerful kingdoms in the Mediterranean. What was not to like? She met his gaze. 'If they have a penchant for patriarchal men with archaic views, then yes, I'd say they'll already be forming a long line to your door.'

His eyes narrowed and for a moment Rosie wondered if she'd gone too far. If he were about to reprimand her for her outspokenness, but he didn't. Instead, he gave her a lazy smile, which was far more lethal than his anger. She didn't want him to smile at her like that—and, of course, she did. She wanted it far too much.

'Are you planning to join us for dinner later?' he questioned. 'Or intending to do another disappearing act?'

'Actually, I'd prefer to have a tray in my room, if that's okay.'

'Actually, it isn't okay,' he said tightly. 'And not just because it's an insult to request *"le sandwich"*, night after night when the embassy chef provides some of the finest cuisine in the city. You are here as part of my delegation so you can damned well put in an appearance, if I command it. Which I do. Do you understand what I'm saying to you, Rosie?' he finished coolly.

'I think you've made yourself pretty clear.'

'In that case, I will take my leave.' He paused and inclined his head. 'But be in no doubt that I like very much the changes you've made to the exhibition.'

'Is that a compliment, Corso?'

'Indeed it is. Accept it with grace.' He gave a cool smile. 'I'll see you at dinner.'

He turned and swept away and Rosie was left gazing after his retreating form, her heart still racing with unwanted longing. As the King's party departed to the flash of affiliated press cameras waiting outside, Phillipe le Clerc made his way back across the room towards her, his dark hair flopping attractively over one eye.

'Mon dieu, le Roi est magnifique!' observed the handsome curator, his voice dropping to an appreciative purr.

'Magnificent indeed,' agreed Rosie woodenly, because how could she possibly deny his words? Yet despite all the jewelled beauty which lay beneath the gleaming glass of the display cabinets, the room seemed empty and lustreless now that Corso had gone. She forced herself to smile at Phillipe. To flick her blonde plait back over her shoulder as if she didn't care about anything other than the upcoming exhibition. 'Shall we just have a last-minute look at the brochures—and then we could grab ourselves a coffee?'

CHAPTER EIGHT

ROSIE WISHED SHE were somewhere else. Anywhere else but here, in this grand embassy dining room in Paris, feeling more awkward than she could ever remember feeling. Yet she had grown up on the periphery of the Monterossian palace, so she was used to fancy surroundings and knew how to feel relatively comfortable in them. But here she couldn't get rid of the sense of being an outsider. An interloper.

Because she was.

Which presumably was why she'd been stuck down at the furthest end of a very long table and about as far from Corso as it was possible to be. She played with the linen napkin on her lap. Of course, she was always going to be seated at the unimportant end of the table! Unless she'd really been expecting to be at the King's right hand—when that honour had been given to the French President's wife, who was nodding her head in blissful agreement with everything Corso was saying.

Rosie tried to smile and listen to the conversation taking place around her. Talking was pretty impossible because her schoolgirl French didn't extend much beyond asking where the bathrooms were. But the general hubbub of the evening was too loud for her to be able to concentrate on anything other than how utterly amazing Corso looked in his Monterossian military regalia, which made the most of his spectacular physique. The dark jacket hugged the broad width of his chest, its row of medals glinting in the guttering light of the candles.

Like every other woman in the room, she had curtseyed when he'd made his grand entrance and then wondered whether she'd imagined his eyes lingering on her as she'd sunk to the marble floor in her silken gown.

The wine was excellent, the food superb. Chandeliers like diamonds suspended in mid-air glittered down on silver cutlery, sparkling crystal, and low bowls of fragrant flowers, which scented the air with heady perfume. But all the pomp and splendour was wasted on her because all Rosie could think about was Corso—like a one-track song playing invasively inside her head.

She pushed away her dish of *Îles flottant*—

untouched mounds of soft meringue, floating in a sea of custard. Such a waste. What was the *matter* with her? It was as though someone had flicked a switch, or cast a spell on her. As if she were in the middle of an enchantment—unable to prevent her gaze from straying to the man who was sitting at the top end of the table. And the mortifying thing was that Corso had actually caught her doing it. Several times, their gazes had locked and the last time it had happened she had flushed, causing the third or fourth secretary—or whatever his position in the embassy was—beside her to remark that they really should improve the air-conditioning in the building.

It didn't help that she was wearing an outfit which made her feel exposed, even though it was probably one of the most modest in the room. A low-cut silvery fitted gown which skimmed her ankles, to allow the peep of gleaming silver stilettos. The stylist had assured Rosie that the dress really suited her and, on one level, she knew it did—she just wasn't used to the brush of silk next to her skin, nor for a lavish borrowed sapphire and diamond necklace and earrings to sparkle like a firework display above her breasts and at her ears. Maybe that was the reason she had let her hair down for once. Usually, she preferred the thick tresses tamed and neat but tonight they tumbled in a newly washed sheen about her bare shoulders, allowing for some welcome concealment.

At least now the toasts and speeches had been made and the guests were following the King's lead and rising from the table. Rosie waited until she was certain she wouldn't be noticed, then slipped away from the banqueting hall, though the relief she had expected to find once back in her suite eluded her.

She sighed. She felt restless. Empty. As if some vital component of her life was missing. An image of flame-kissed hair and amber-flecked eyes taunted the edge of her consciousness—and she wondered how she was going to get any sleep tonight.

Kicking off the silver shoes, she removed the necklace and earrings and put them in the safe, before padding barefoot over to the window to stare out at the Eiffel Tower. Dominating the Parisian skyline, the enormous structure was lit with coloured lights, which were reflected on the wide stretch of the river Seine, and which flashed like fireworks into the bedroom.

She went into the bathroom to brush her teeth and was just thinking about getting undressed when she heard a light tap at the door.

She frowned as she spat some peppermint foam into the sink. Who would come looking for her at this time of night? Would the embassy have thought to send up a cup of late-night hot chocolate? Unlikely.

She opened the door and her heart thudded because Corso was standing there, still in his military uniform. Vibrant and handsome and oozing sex appeal, the King of Monterosso was standing on *her* doorstep. She should have felt nervous, or outraged, or indignant, or angry or... But she felt none of those things. The only thing which was fizzing through her veins was the overwhelming certainty that there was nobody else in the world she would rather see. But Corso must not know that. Definitely not. She must remain calm. In control. Maybe he was here to discuss an aspect of the exhibition he'd forgotten to mention earlier.

'Goodness,' she said coolly, clutching the door handle tightly for support and hoping he didn't notice. 'This is unexpected.'

For a moment Corso couldn't bring himself to answer.

He hadn't been able to keep his eyes off her during the formal dinner. Unassuming Rosie Forrester—who seemed to have become a thorn in his flesh. He'd registered her curvy body clothed in a gown the colour of starlight. He'd been mesmerised by the lustrous fall of hair cascading down around her shoulders and the alluring flush of pink in her cheeks. There had been a captivating air about her, which had set her apart from everyone else in the room— a watchfulness and solitude he had found completely mesmerising. Had that been deliberate? Was she aware that those wordless looks she'd been directing at him had made it impossible for him to concentrate on a word the French President's wife had been saying? And now she was standing in front of him like some incandescent angel in her silver gown. 'Can I come in?' he questioned throatily.

'Really?' she verified, with a slightly bemused rise of her eyebrows.

Outraged that she should have the temerity to challenge a question which would have made any other woman melt, he glared. 'Yes, really. Unless you wish to have this conversation with me on your doorstep, which would not only be extremely indiscreet in the circumstances—but also highly discourteous.'

'Oh. We're having a conversation, are we?' she questioned, but she opened the door wider all the same, allowing him to step inside, and then closed it quietly behind him. She headed towards a tall lamp and switched it on in a very busy manner, before turning to look at him, her eyebrows still raised. 'Okay. What do you want to talk about? The exhibition? The dinner? It all seemed to go very well tonight and I thought your speech was great, if that's what you're... Corso?' The prattle of her nervous words halted and she looked at him in confusion, as if she had only just noticed the tension in his face and body. 'Is something the matter?'

'I just think we need to establish a few boundaries,' he said unevenly. And since he was aware that visiting her room at close to midnight was almost certainly in direct breach of the boundaries he was about to propose, he moved as far away from her as possible.

'Right,' she said slowly, still with that faint look of perplexity. 'Go on, then. Let's hear them.'

For a moment Corso's resolve faltered because, in the apricot light spilling from the lamp, her lips were parted and her eyes were glittering like dark stars. That unbelievable hair was brushing against her cheeks and he found himself wanting to use one of those pale, silken strands as an anchor. To wind it round his finger and use it to draw her face close to his, so that he could kiss her. He wanted to kiss her so much. Angrily, he pushed the thought away but traces of it lingered in his mind.

Was it seven years of self denial which made him answer her with such a marked lack of finesse? 'It's infuriating, but I can't stop thinking about you.'

He saw her brief look of uncertainty before she shrugged. 'Well, we go back a long way, don't we?'

'That's not what I'm talking about.'

'No. I guess not.' Suddenly all the uncertainty was gone. Her gaze was clear and he was reminded of the focus she had demonstrated when she'd been showing him around the exhibition earlier. 'Perhaps you'd like to tell me exactly what it is you *are* talking about.'

'With pleasure.' He could have kicked himself for his inappropriate choice of word as she stood there, bathed in the light from the Eiffel Tower. 'It isn't going to happen, Rosie.'

'What isn't?'

'Please.' He didn't bother to keep the impatience from his voice. 'We're not teenagers. Let's at least be honest with ourselves. We need to work and travel together and at the moment I'm not finding it particularly easy to do either.'

'Why not?'

'You know damned well why,' he gritted

out. 'Unless you are denying the chemistry between us?'

She blushed. She actually *blushed*. 'Wouldn't acknowledging it be a teeny bit presumptuous, Corso?'

'So you feel it, too?' His words were a silken challenge.

'Yes, of course I do,' she admitted and pulled a face which made him think of a younger Rosie. 'I find you extremely attractive. Along with every other woman with a pulse, no doubt. It's a pity really. All those years of not understanding what anyone saw in you seem to have come to nothing—which is annoying to say the least. Happy now?'

Happy was the last adjective he would have used to describe his current state of being. Frustrated? Yes. Aching? Certainly. Resentful? Possibly. 'I agree, it's…annoying.' He paused. 'But you do realise that nothing is going to happen.'

Her brow clouded. 'So you just said, although you haven't made yourself very clear.'

Afterwards he would justify his next remark by convincing himself she'd goaded him into it. 'We're not going to have sex.'

'Have sex?' she echoed, the cadence of her voice rising in disbelief. 'Have you taken leave of your mind, Corso? I don't want to have sex with you!'

'Oh, really?' he challenged, but deep down he knew his challenge was layered with provocation. 'You're either distorting the truth or deluding yourself if you think that, Rosie.'

She flew at him then—and wasn't that exactly what he wanted? Her blonde hair was streaming like a banner behind her as she hurled herself against him, her balled fists drumming uselessly at his chest, and he felt a jolt of something he didn't recognise as he stared down at the pale gleam of her head. He suspected she wanted a physical outlet for her rage, and couldn't decide whether to let her just get it out of her system, or capture one of her wrists before telling her to calm down. But her fists were no longer drumming, they were kneading at his flesh in a way which was distracted yet inciting, and he was no longer trying to decide how to react. Because suddenly he couldn't help himself. He could battle with himself no longer. Or maybe he had just surrendered because he was no longer thinking, just *feeling*.

Heeding nothing but the siren call of her body, he pulled her into his arms, her breathless gasp of assent reinforced by the way she was reaching up to cling to his shoulders, as though he wasn't the only one in need of an anchor. Impatiently, he brushed her hair aside and began to kiss her. His tongue teased her lips apart and she was the most delicious thing he had ever tasted—coffee and toothpaste and something else, something which was uniquely her. Something which made him grow even harder. Her breasts were pushing against his chest—their tips like diamond bullets pushing against the delicate fabric of her gown. He made one last attempt to resist—at least, that was what he tried to tell himself—but her soft moan of incitement made resistance impossible. He felt like a man who'd been lost in the desert, stumbling upon a deep well of cool water and being told he wasn't allowed to drink. As he deepened the kiss, he found his hand straying towards her breast and she gripped his shoulders even tighter. Was that his name she was whimpering?

He cupped her breast, his thumb circling the thrusting nipple, and never had he wanted to lick and suck an area of skin so badly.

'Corso,' she gasped.

'You want this?'

'So much. I can't… I can't tell you how much.'

And neither could he. It was because it had

been so long since he'd had sex that his heart felt as if it were on fire. It must be. His hands skated hungrily over the contours of her body— firm curves covered by the soft silk which defined them. She writhed as he stroked her, the subtle, almost indefinable scent of her desire filling the air and reminding his starved body of everything he'd been missing. He knew if he touched her she would be wet. Just as if she touched him, she would find him rock-hard. He swallowed. He had to have her. It seemed as inevitable as the sun which rose every morning over the red mountains of Monterosso. Yet surely to do so would be the height of recklessness?

He didn't care. The only thing he cared about right then was the pressure of her lips as they kissed frantically. He could never remember a kiss like this—so deep, so drugging, so unbelievably *erotic*. His fingers were tangled in her hair. He pressed his body against hers and she whispered his name. He pushed her up against the wall and felt her thighs part. And he knew then that he could take her. That she wanted him to take her.

'Rosie,' he husked.

'Yes,' she breathed. 'Yes.'

It was an answer and an incitement melded

into one delicious word and Corso bent to clasp the hem of her dress. The fabric trickled like liquid silk over his hand as he began to ruck the gown up, eager to tease his finger against her molten heat until she pulsed helplessly beneath him. But he tried to pace himself. To spin it out for as long as possible in order to luxuriate in these long-forgotten feelings of lust.

And then, just as abruptly, he stopped, his hand coming to a halt on the jut of her knee which caused her to make a slurred objection. His heart was crashing against his ribcage as the unwanted voice of reason began to clamour inside his head, asking if this was how seven years of denial were going to end.

He let the hem of her dress fall back down. 'We're not going to do this,' he ground out.

Her eyes looked huge and troubled and dis-appointed. 'We're…we're not?'

'No.' He saw she was trembling and ap-peared unsteady on her feet and Corso con-vinced himself it was simply courtesy which made him lift her up and carry her towards the large bed he had avoided looking at when he'd first entered the room.

She was lighter than he had expected and he missed her warm weight as he laid her down against the snowy white counterpane. But this was the right thing to do. They weren't teenagers and there was no reason for them to behave that way—fumbling at each other's clothes, then having sex because they couldn't stop themselves. He had called a halt to it just in time and he should commend himself for his steely self-control.

But her pale hair was spread like moonlight over the pillow and he wanted to stroke it. And her lips were parted and he wanted to touch them with his own.

'I should go,' he said.

With the tip of one finger, she reached up to trace the outline of his mouth and never had such a simple gesture felt so powerfully hypnotic. Damn you, Rosie Forrester, he thought resentfully. *Damn* you.

'Go, then. If that's what you want.'

He could barely breathe, let alone speak. 'You know damned well it's not.'

There was a pause. 'Well, then.'

Deliberately, Rosie made her comment sound like an invitation, or an acceptance—it all depended on how you looked at it. But inside she was praying and hoping as she saw an agony of indecision distorting Corso's carved features and she wondered which way he would go. Deep down she knew he didn't really want this, and on one level neither did she. Because nothing but trouble was going to come from it. Instinctively, she recognised that. Every sensible atom of her body was urging her to send him away, and she had spent most of her life being sensible.

Yet tonight Corso Andrea da Vignola had ignited something in her. Something which was making her body ache with an unbearable kind of longing. It wasn't so much about wanting him—it was more about *needing* him and feeling that the rest of her life would seem incomplete if she didn't have him. She wanted him to douse the flames of desire which were threatening to consume her. To free her from the burden of never having tasted physical pleasure before—a burden which grew heavier with every year that passed.

But it was his call.

It had to be.

'I don't have any condoms with me,' he said.

His words were the antithesis of romance and his brutal declaration should have been enough to kill Rosie's passion stone-dead, but, ironically, they made her feel more comfortable. Because he wasn't pretending. He wasn't saying stuff he didn't mean in order to get her into bed. He wasn't talking about moonlight and roses, he was talking about contraception. It felt like a grown-up thing they were engaged in—a very adult way of approaching sex.

'I do,' she said.

She saw his look of surprise and, yes, disappointment—he didn't manage to disguise that in time and she didn't know whether to be pleased or insulted at his silent judgement. But it didn't matter whether he thought she was being bold, or whether it wasn't the 'done thing' for a woman to be quite so assertive. She wasn't seeking his good opinion of her. She just wanted him so badly that she felt she might die if she couldn't have him.

'Where?' he demanded.

She ought to fetch them herself, but the thought of getting up from this bed—exquisitely aroused as she was—to parade in front of him in her unfamiliar evening gown was more than she could bear. Better she was lying here if he changed his mind.

'In the back of the wardrobe,' she said breathlessly, 'is my suitcase. They're in a little red purse in the inside section.'

He found the suitcase and flipped it open, frowning for a moment as he saw the neat piles of clothes. 'Why haven't you unpacked?'

'Because they're my normal clothes. You

know. The ones which were deemed redundant after your stylist provided me with a new wardrobe for the royal tour.'

For a moment Rosie wondered if she'd said too much. If her sarcastic words would reinforce the difference between them and remind him of how eminently unsuitable she was to be the King's lover. But wasn't she jumping the gun? She wasn't his lover yet and she still might not be. Not when he was regarding the pack of condoms with an expression of bemusement.

'Are these still in date?'

'Of course.' No way was she going to start explaining why she was carrying them around, because he had started to undress and every sane thought flew straight out of her mind. He took off his military jacket and hung it on the back of the chair. Next came the long, polished boots—so that all he was left wearing were his dark trousers with the scarlet stripe down the sides and a close-fitting shirt of white silk. He came back to the bed and sat on the edge of it, his free hand stroking her cheek with a hypnotic movement, before tracing the outline of her lips so that they trembled beneath his touch.

'Now,' he said.

Too unsure of herself to know how to react, she suspected she was probably much too passive as he peeled the dress from her body, his gaze roving appreciatively over the delicate lace of her new push-up bra and matching French knickers, which he removed so slowly that she wanted to urge him to hurry up. But when he bent his head to lick at each exposed nipple he gave a groan which sounded almost help-less and Rosie began to feel a sense of her own power growing alongside her mounting excite-ment. Her inhibitions melted like butter in the midday sun and soon she was unbuttoning his silk shirt and spreading her fingers with glo-rious abandon over the warm, beating satin of his chest.

He made a little sound in the back of his throat as he began to unbutton his trousers, be-fore briefly kicking them away. And it occurred to her—though only briefly—that the King's military clothes really ought not to be lying in a crumpled heap on a bedroom floor, but by then Corso was back on the bed and pulling her in his arms and kissing her, and the concern flew straight out of her head.

Dimly, she was aware of him reaching for the protection he had retrieved from her suitcase but by then nothing else mattered other than thinking she would explode if he carried on stroking her like that. She thought that, compared to her own sense of wild abandon, his own movements seemed to be cloaked in an element of fierce control. His face was a shadowed mask she could not read and his lips were hard and tense.

He took her to the brink so many times before at last he entered her with one long, deep thrust and Rosie couldn't hold back her small cry, which was more about rapture than pain. He stilled only fractionally, his narrowed eyes glinting, before continuing with those long and incredible thrusts.

It came upon her when she wasn't expecting it. When she was so lost in the experience that she relaxed enough to let go. She'd read about it, of course. Descriptions of starbursts and fireworks she'd always considered slightly fanciful. But not any more. If anything, they were understatements. As she began to spasm around him, Rosie felt as if she were being sucked up in a warm jet stream to the top of the mountain, before tumbling blissfully back down to earth again. And that was when the King's own movements became more rapid. She felt his powerful body jerk as his head fell back and the cry which erupted from his lips was like nothing she'd ever heard. But he drove his mouth down on hers in a hard kiss, as if he wanted to disguise the sound—and for the first time, Rosie wondered where his bodyguards were.

For a while everything felt perfect. She wrapped her arms tightly around his back, with her head resting against the broad width of his shoulder. Almost absently she dropped a kiss onto the satiny skin there and, almost immediately, she felt his body tense as he withdrew from her.

She tried to convince herself it was normal for a man to roll to the opposite side of the bed after having sex with a woman for the first time, but instinct was contradicting her because there was something about Corso's body language which warned her that whatever was coming next was probably going to be unwelcome.

Because his expression had darkened, and he was actually *scowling*, and Rosie wondered what had caused him to look that way. Maybe she had been a disappointment. Maybe he was already regretting it. Until she told herself to stop being so *wet*. If she had been confident enough to point him into the direction of a packet of condoms, then surely it was pointless to shrink back into the shadows now.

She wriggled back against the pillows. 'Is something wrong?'

'Wrong? Doesn't that qualify for understatement of the year?' He gave a bitter laugh. 'You mean, other than that it was your first time and you didn't bother to tell me?'

CHAPTER NINE

CORSO TENSED AS he waited for Rosie's answer, trying to ignore her pink and blonde beauty as she lay back against the pillows. Ravishing Rosie. Rumpled Rosie. Innocent Rosie. His groin tightened and he willed the exquisite aching to subside because this kind of thinking wasn't helpful.

'Why should I have told you it was my first time?' she demanded. 'I'm not sure how these things work because I'm a novice—obviously. Is it a prerequisite of having sex that you're supposed to run through a list of your previous partners first? Bit of a passion-killer, I would have thought. Anyway, it's not a big deal.'

Corso grabbed the bedsheet and hauled it over his throbbing groin, unwilling to let her see the evidence of his rapidly growing desire. He felt a multiplicity of emotions. Sated, yes. But he felt baffled too—and more than a little angry with her. And with himself. Because, without putting too fine a point on it—why her?

Having successfully resisted the lure of women far more appropriate than Rosie Forrester during the past seven years, he was wondering what had made him fall so eagerly into her bed just now. Maybe it was just a question of timing. Or the need for distraction as the meeting with his brother approached. Was that why all his control and determination seemed to have deserted him? He had hungered for her, and she for him—but she had neglected to tell him something vitally important. Why had she done that? To trap him?

Pernicious guilt washed over him, for no way could he underplay his own role in what had just happened. On the contrary. He should have *known* she was innocent. Should have guessed. Should have run a mile from the indefinable allure she exuded and which had so effectively snared him. Were the clues there all the time and lust had simply blinded him to them? Or had he allowed their undeniable camaraderie to gnaw away at his defences, leaving him so vulnerable to her voluptuous blonde beauty that seven years of celibacy had been annihilated in the space of a few minutes?

'Don't try to be funny, because you're not

succeeding,' he snapped. 'Of course it's a big deal. You were a virgin, for God's sake.'

'But everyone's a virgin at some point in their life,' she pointed out. 'Even you. When did you first have sex, Corso? Why don't we talk about *that*?'

Impatiently, he shook his head. It was so long ago that he could barely remember the details. Only that the woman had been older and had known every damned trick in the book. And it had felt nothing like this. Nothing ever had. *And wasn't that the most galling thing of all?* That this innocent young woman he'd known since she barely reached his elbow should have brought him to his knees. 'Don't change the subject, Rosie,' he snapped. 'I'm still waiting for an explanation.'

'Which I don't believe I'm contractually obliged to give you.'

He almost laughed but glared instead. 'I'm waiting,' he said, in his most frosty and regal tone.

She breathed out an unsteady sigh and shrugged her bare shoulders. 'It just never happened for me, that's all. Mum…she needed a lot of support when we first moved back to England, so there was always that. Obviously, I've been asked out on dates before but none of them, well…obviously none of them progressed to the stage where I might have been tempted to take it further.' She pushed a handful of hair away from her flushed cheek. 'You didn't guess?'

Corso didn't trust himself to answer immediately—afraid that to do so might reveal too much, for it was beginning to dawn on him that he behaved differently with her than he did with anyone else. Perhaps because he had known her as well as a prince could know any commoner—at a time in their lives before duty or age had imposed their particular demands on him. Just after his mother had died, when he had undoubtedly been vulnerable, she and her family had helped him sample a simpler life. And yes, he'd caught a glimpse of her undoubted innocence at his birthday ball—with her gawky and ungainly appearance—but he'd been so busy being angry with her that he'd imagined such a stage was only transitory.

One of the reasons he had considered her the perfect candidate for this role—apart from her undoubted knowledge of the subject—was because he'd never really thought of her as a *woman*. She had been the sweet daughter of his mentor. The girl who always had her head in a book. He certainly hadn't been prepared for the tangible sexiness she exuded when he'd come to find her in England, even though she'd been wearing the most unflattering clothes he'd ever seen. Or for her behaviour when he'd turned up at her suite tonight.

'Nobody would expect a virgin to conveniently produce packs of condoms!' he snapped.

'Really?' Lying back against the pillows, she cushioned her head against her folded arms. 'I thought that was the way things were done. Of course women must take responsibility for contraception and not just leave it up to the man. So why not carry some around—just in case?'

'Is that the reason you had them, Rosie?' he questioned moodily. *Just in case?*

She shrugged again and he wished she hadn't because it made her magnificent breasts wiggle in a way which made him want to lick his tongue all over them.

'Actually, my sister gave them to me as a part of my birthday present, as a joke. Only it wasn't really a joke.' She hesitated. 'She thought it was time I started doing things that other women of my age were doing.'

'So you chose me as your initiation project?' His mouth thinned. 'Aiming a little high, weren't you?'

'Actually—' indignantly, she sat up in bed to

glare at him and the flicker of fire in her eyes was uncomfortably attractive '—ignoring the unbelievable arrogance of your last remark, I could say that you chose me. Or that we chose each other. This thing has been building between us for days now—even innocent little me was aware of that. Though I wouldn't have done anything about it—on principle—and not just because your guards make it impossible for anyone to get near you. You were the one who made the running, remember?'

'I came to warn you off,' he raged.

'Of course you did, Corso. You came to my room at midnight and told me we weren't going to have sex, before taking off your clothes.' Her lips twitched, as if she was trying not to smile. 'But what's happened has happened and there's no need to worry about it. I know how these things work. I've lived around royals for long enough. I'm not expecting to become your queen.'

'Because that would never happen!'

'Obviously. Even if I wanted it to—which I don't—you helpfully spelled it out for me in words of one syllable just the other day. I know you'll be marrying a royal princess some time soon. Lucky woman!' She pinned a smile to her

lips. 'So why can't we look on what just happened as a very enjoyable interlude?'

Corso stilled. 'A *very enjoyable interlude*?'
he echoed softly. 'Am I now to be damned with
faint praise?'

'I didn't mean it that way.'

'No?'

'No!' Some of her bravado left her and she
hesitated, not looking at him now, but staring down at the edge of the sheet, which she
was rubbing between her finger and thumb.
'It was…amazing, if you must know. Totally
amazing. For me, anyway.'

'For me, too,' he said into the silence which
followed, then wondered why on earth he had
been so unnecessarily transparent. Because she
was inexperienced, that was why. Surely it was
only fair to reassure her—so that with future
lovers she would be filled with confidence in
her own sexuality. And then Corso scowled,
unprepared for the territorial twist of jealousy
which clenched at his gut at the thought of her
being in the arms of another man.

'I'm just surprised…'

'Mmm?' he said distractedly as her words
broke into his uncomfortable reverie.

She looked up from her study of the sheet,
her teeth digging into the rosy cushion of her

bottom lip. 'I'm surprised you chose me, that's all. There must be loads of other women who would have made a much more suitable sexual partner. Why me?'

This was usually the kind of thing a woman asked when she was fishing for a compliment, but Corso suspected that wasn't true in this case. He thought about ignoring her question—of deftly batting it away, confident in the knowledge that nobody ever asked a king something twice. But Rosie was different. She had known him before he'd acceded to the throne. She'd once seen him with tear-bright eyes and when he'd complained about the grit which had flown in them while out riding, she had simply squeezed his arm, before swiftly dropping her hand, as if remembering that she had no right to touch the monarch. She hadn't ever mentioned it again. She hadn't come out with endless platitudes about how sorry she was for the loss of his mother and he had been grateful to her for that, because he had been hurting badly.

But she was no longer that young girl, running on instinct and innocence. She was a woman in her prime—poised on the brink of discovering the rich world of her own sexuality. Didn't he owe her the truth? 'You want to know why I couldn't resist you?' he questioned.

'I'm curious.'

He hesitated. 'You are obviously very attractive.'

'But not your usual type?'

'Well, no.' It had been so long since he'd had a 'type' that Corso found himself wondering whether his preferences might have changed over the years. 'If you really want an explanation, I guess you'd have to put it down to proximity.'

'Proximity?' she echoed, unable to keep the tang of disappointment from her voice. 'And that's all?'

Yes, of course that was all. Close contact plus rampaging hormones equalled explosive physical chemistry. It was no more complex than that. She needed to understand that. And he needed to understand it, too. 'And when proximity is mixed with abstinence—it makes a very potent cocktail. You see, I haven't been intimate with a woman for a very long time, Rosie,' he added huskily. 'Not for over seven years, in fact. Ring any bells?'

It took a few seconds before she answered and he saw the confusion clear from her face as she nodded. 'You're talking about that woman I overheard just before your party?' she breathed. 'What was her name?'

'I don't remember.'

'Tiffany!' she said triumphantly. 'That was it. Tiffany Sackler. I warned you that she was telling a friend she wanted to have your baby. And you were very angry with me.'

'I was more angry with myself,' he admitted.

'And that was enough to put you off sex?'

'It didn't *put me off* sex. It made me re-evaluate my life. It made me consider that maybe I hadn't been thinking through my position properly. I realised I had been placing myself in an invidious position and could easily be compromised by people whose motives were not, shall we say…pure.'

'And was it very hard?' she ventured. 'To go without sex for so long?'

'Hard would not be my adjective of choice,' he commented drily, a reluctant smile tugging at the edges of his mouth. 'You know, you really are going to have to stop blushing like that when you're in bed with me. It's really very distracting.'

'I'm serious,' she said, seeming to hesitate before forging on. 'It's just quite a lot to take on board because you were so well known for being a…'

'A what, Rosie?' he challenged.

She clasped her fingers together. 'A sex symbol, I suppose. A bit of a player. It must have been like a chocoholic deciding they weren't going to eat sugar for the foreseeable.'

He stared out of the window, where the Eiffel Tower was currently lit up with the purple and turquoise colours of the Monterossian flag, as it had been since his arrival in France. 'If you must know, at first I enjoyed the discipline of self-denial. I have always enjoyed testing myself, especially when it's difficult. It's like basic training when you're in the military. No one wants to get out of bed at six a.m. and take an icy shower, before running miles with a heavy pack on your back—but that's what makes your body into a powerful machine. Abstinence helped keep my mind focussed and it coincided with my accession to the throne, and the discovery of exactly what I had inherited.'

This time she didn't prompt him. Not even when he couldn't prevent his voice from distorting with the vein of bitterness he usually kept buried deep inside him. She just tucked a strand of pale hair behind her ear and gazed at him and he thought how much of her father there was in her—for didn't she seem to share his uncanny ability of knowing when to speak and when to remain silent?

And suddenly he found himself telling her. Not all of it, no, but some. Some things he would never tell. 'Countries are like people,' he ground out. 'They evolve and grow. And I didn't like the country which mine had become. The world had moved on and the casinos, which were licensed a long time ago, had begun to attract the worst kinds of people. When I looked closely, I discovered an underbelly which sickened me. Money-laundering. Prostitution. Drugs.' He saw her wince. 'I knew I had to bring about a profound change. I wanted to make Monterosso into a beacon of sustainability and culture. So I shut down some of the more dubious establishments, poured money into social projects and rewilded many of our forests. I knew we had the potential to become a World Heritage site, if we could just clean up our act.'

'That's a pretty incredible thing you've done,' she put in eagerly. 'And that's why you wanted to show the Forrester artefacts to the world.'

Her eyes looked so shining and full of life and in that moment she appeared so utterly idealistic—and, yes, *beautiful*—that Corso couldn't bring himself to disillusion her about his motives. He had told her enough. More than enough. He knew only too well that information was power and was wary of allowing her to get any closer than she already was. Physical proximity was one thing, but anything else had the potential to be problematic. For her, rather than him. He didn't want verbal confidences to be mistaken for real intimacy, because there was only one kind of intimacy he could guarantee. And maybe it was about time he demonstrated that to her, so there could be no mistake.

'Come here,' he said silkily.

He saw the indecision which flickered over her flushed face and he wondered if she recognised the significance of his request. Because this wasn't about him reaching out to her, even though it would have been ridiculously easy to pull her into his arms and kiss her and have her moaning his name before a minute had elapsed. She had to come to *him*. To acquiesce and to relinquish power to him. If she wanted this, then she needed to play by his rules—for he had been born to rule.

He watched as her eyes darkened and then, with her magnificent breasts swaying a little, she slid across the bed towards him, her body warm and soft as it collided with the hard muscle of his.

'What do you want?' she murmured, wrapping her arms around his neck and pressing herself against him.

Corso's body was programmed to respond

instantly to a question like that, and it did. He thought how quickly a woman could learn to be a coquette when a man had satisfied her, and he smiled as he trickled his fingers down over her breast and felt her nipple pucker. 'That isn't a very imaginative question,' he chided. 'I would have expected something better from you, Rosie.'

'Don't they say that people who have expectations are doomed to be disappointed?'

'I promise that disappointment is something you'll never experience when you're in bed with me.'

'That is so…' Her eyelids fluttered to a close. 'So…'

'So what?' he teased, his hand now moving down beyond her belly.

'Egotistical,' she managed, at last. 'Corso! What…what are you doing?'

'I think you know very well what I'm doing. I'm going to have sex with you again because last time was your first time and I feel it's my duty to convince you that the pleasure you experienced wasn't a fluke.'

'You're…you're making it sound like some sort of power game,' she whispered.

He didn't answer. Just dipped his head down past her navel and a rush of carnal satisfaction flooded through him as his tongue found her moist bud. He made her come twice more—with his finger and with his mouth—but still he didn't allow himself the luxury of his own release. He could feel the heightening of tension, the terrible aching at his groin, but still he resisted entering her until she was begging him to. As if he wanted to demonstrate to them both that he had clawed back that steely control which had kept him celibate all these years. That he was still in charge and always would be.

Briefly he relinquished his hold on her when at last he could bear it no more, and reached for a condom.

'Corso?' she questioned, and he could see she was looking at him with something like concern in her eyes. But he said nothing. He didn't want any more analysis, or questions, or explanations. That had never been his way. He didn't want to confront his own feelings, or to question hers. He wanted to be deep inside her and lose himself completely in her tight wet heat and only after that would he consider what happened next.

But when it was all over and he lay there, drained and satisfied, he was overcome by a sudden air of melancholy he couldn't seem to shift. He turned on his side to study her and his heart missed a beat. One arm was splayed above her head in unconscious abandon and her head was pillowed on the pale silk of her hair. Oh, Rosie, he thought sadly, as he looked down at her sleeping face and the soft lashes which feathered her pink cheeks. Far better that you'd kicked me out last night and told me never to darken your door again.

CHAPTER TEN

WHEN ROSIE WOKE next morning, she wondered if she'd dreamt the whole thing. She opened her eyes. The unshuttered windows showed a cloudy spring day, the Eiffel Tower looking more sombre without its night-time glitter of flashing lights. Last night it had looked like an extravagant fairground illumination. Today it was just a giant grey construction of metal.

She looked around the bedroom, as if searching for evidence that Corso had been here last night, making delicious love to her. Or, more accurately, introducing her to sex. Because there was a big difference between the two, and only a fool would forget that.

But there was nothing of him to be seen. The military jacket was no longer hanging on the back of a chair—nor the scarlet striped dark trousers lying in a hastily discarded heap at the side of the bed. Not a single sign that the King of Monterosso had been there. She licked her lips, because his presence still permeated the room all the same. She could detect his faint scent on her skin. And inside she was warm and aching from where he had been deep inside her.

She must have fallen asleep because she hadn't heard him leave. There had been no farewell kiss. No promises made, or awkward conversation before he took his leave. Should she be grateful for that? She picked up her watch, which was lying on the locker beside the bed, and saw it was just gone seven.

Now what?

More than anything she needed to get ready to go to work, so she lifted the phone to ask for coffee to be delivered to her suite. It arrived accompanied by the most delicious croissant she'd ever tasted—at least she'd got her appetite back—and soon she was feeling a bit more like herself, rather than someone who had temporarily lost sight of her place in the world. But as Rosie showered and dressed in another museum-suitable outfit, she couldn't help mulling over the surprising things Corso had told her last night. About taking a vow of chastity—which was essentially what it amounted to—after she'd confided what she'd overheard all those years ago. And then pouring his redirected energy into polishing the tarnished reputation of his beloved country and putting it back on track.

She didn't want to hang around the embassy, looking as though she were waiting or expecting something—because surely it would be easier if she just made herself scarce. Less embarrassing that way. She didn't want Corso to feel responsible for her, or to worry about how she was going to react. She wasn't going to blush, or sulk, or melt into a heap when he swept through the embassy with his entourage. She was going to take what had happened completely in her stride. She was going to be modern. After all, Paris was one of the most sophisticated places in the world—so why not allow herself to be influenced by it?

Noticed only by a couple of staff, she slipped from the residence and caught the Metro to the Jardin des Tuileries and went inside the museum to look for Phillipe. She found him in the office, his head bent over one of the Parisian broadsheets, and he looked up and smiled as she entered, that lock of dark hair flopping attractively into one eye. *'Bonjour,'* he murmured as he pointed to the paper. 'Have you seen this?'

She hadn't. Rosie blinked with surprise as

she peered over his shoulder. On the front page was a photo of her, next to one of Corso—both taken at last night's dinner, when she'd been only half aware of a photographer capturing the embassy event for posterity. It was hard to recognise herself. The designer clothes and the jewels glittering at her ears and throat made her look like an expensive stranger. And her *hair*. Would she really have worn it that way if she'd realised it was going to tumble to her waist and look so untamed?

'What does it say?' she asked Phillipe.

He scanned the text. 'It talks about the King's plans for closer ties between our two countries. It mentions at some length your family's long-standing relationship with the da Vignola line and remarks on how beautiful you are. *C'est vrai, chérie,*' he affirmed, when she made a muffled sound of protest. 'You are. And then it talks about the exhibition, and that we will be open later this morning.' He smiled. 'I think we are going to be very busy today, Rosie.'

Phillipe wasn't exaggerating and there was a long line in place before the doors had even opened. But Rosie was furious with herself for feeling a distinct air of disappointment as the day wore on. She kept looking up to scan the entrance, or making an excuse to go to the front desk so she could peer outside and see if the King's car was anywhere to be seen. But it wasn't. And neither was he.

They closed at six and Phillipe invited her to join him and the other staff for a celebratory glass of champagne in a bar around the corner, but Rosie refused. She honestly didn't think she could paste a bright smile to her face any longer and she certainly didn't feel like celebrating.

She wished she were back in her little cottage in the woods but, since that wasn't on the cards, at least she could go back to her suite at the embassy and come to terms with the fact that last night had been a one-off. A big mistake—at least, on Corso's part. He was probably regretting having broken his sexual fast with her, rather than someone amazing and well connected, and famous. But the last thing she was going to do was to fixate on the King. She needed to remind herself that this was the first time she'd ever been in Paris and to make the most of it, because a few weeks from now and she'd be back on the railway.

Pulling out her guidebook, she went for a walk in the Tuileries gardens, thinking how peaceful it was to have this beautiful space, right in the middle of one of the busiest cities in the world. Yet somehow, the sight of the tulips and frothy blossom and the stunning pink of the Judas trees gave the place an air of something unbearably poignant. What *was* it about springtime which made people start thinking about love? wondered Rosie. Love was nothing but a word. A stupid word. People bandied it around and used it when it suited them, for all kinds of reasons. A random stranger had said it to her mother and because of that she'd given away all her life savings. Her dad had loved his work and because of that, he had taken a risk which had ultimately killed him.

Pushing her troubled thoughts away, she strolled around the gardens until the light began to fade, before catching the Metro—and when she arrived back inside the embassy it was to see Rodrigo, the King's aide, heading towards her, a resolute expression on his face.

'The King requests your company, Miss Forrester,' he said, before she'd even had a chance to take her coat off.

'When?'

'Now.'

'I need to change first,' she said calmly, refusing to be intimidated by Rodrigo's faint frown. She wasn't a well-trained dog who would go running whenever the King whistled! More than that, she wanted to be in control. To impose something of her own agenda onto what was happening, rather than fall in with everything Corso wanted. Because suddenly she was scared. Scared of the way he could make her feel—and even more scared of what could happen if she allowed herself to fall for him.

That was never going to happen.

Because she must never allow it to happen.

'I will wait,' Rodrigo said repressively, standing sentry outside her door.

Rosie took as long as she dared to remove the fine wool trousers and silk shirt she'd worn for work, deliberately rejecting all the other gorgeous clothes hanging inside her wardrobe. She didn't want to wear anything the stylist had chosen. Not now, in her downtime—before a face-to-face with a man she should never have had sex with. She needed to look like herself. To *feel* like herself. Which was why she pulled on a pair of faded jeans and teamed them with an ancient sweater she'd knitted during one of those long winter's nights at the hospital, when her father had been lying in his coma.

Rodrigo hadn't moved from his position outside her door, the narrowing of his eyes his only reaction to her dressed-down appearance. As she followed him to the King's suite on the first floor, Rosie felt like a prisoner being escorted to the cells. But the room he showed her into was nothing like a cell—its gilded splendour indicating the importance of its inhabitant, who stood silhouetted against the window as he stared down at the Rue du Faubourg Saint-Honoré. He turned round as he heard them enter and Rosie's heart gave a powerful leap as she met the gleam of his eyes and memories of last night came rushing back in an erotic flood.

'Miss Forrester, Your Royal Highness,' murmured the King's aide.

'Yes, I can see that for myself,' said Corso impatiently. 'Leave us now, Rodrigo, will you? I don't wish to be disturbed until I give the order. Understand?'

'Perfectly, my liege.'

There was silence even after Rodrigo had slipped from the room and the two of them just remained staring at each another, as if it were the first time they'd ever met.

Corso waited for Rosie's reaction, his impatience growing when still she didn't speak. Because didn't part of him—a big part—want her to rebuke him? To ask why he had slipped from her suite without fanfare and demand to know what he was going to do next? Or even to complain about him sending an aide to es-

cort her here instead of going to find her himself. Because wouldn't that have given him the
chance to snap back that she had no right to
make demands on him, that she should know
her place?

But she didn't. She spoke not one word. Just
subjected him to a coolly speculative stare,
which was doing dangerous things to his blood
pressure. She was very controlled, he thought,
with reluctant admiration. And she handled
herself very well, looking bizarrely at home
in these lavish surroundings, despite wearing
the most outrageously old jeans and sweater.

'You say nothing,' he observed.

'I am waiting for your lead, Your Royal Highness.' Her answer was demure but he couldn't
mistake the tinge of mockery which underpinned it. 'Isn't that the correct procedure?'

'To hell with procedure,' he said, unable to
prevent himself from walking across the room
and pulling her into his arms. He looked down
into the silvery gleam of her eyes and saw her
pupils darken and his body responded instantly.
'You've been away much too long.'

'I've been...' Her breathing had quick-
ened. 'I've been working at the museum all
day, which is, after all, what I'm being paid to

do. We've had a gratifying number of people through the door, just in case you're interested.'

'Yet you chose to walk alone in the Jardin des Tuileries afterwards, rather than join your colleagues for a drink?' he mused. 'Was Phillipe very disappointed by that, do you think?'

She frowned. 'How do you know what I did, and what does Phillipe have to do with anything?'

He shrugged, his fingers straying beneath her sweater to encounter the warmth of flesh beneath, wanting to distract her with his touch rather than admit that he had been bothered by an uncharacteristic twist of jealousy. 'I had a couple of my bodyguards keep an eye on you.'

'Ah!' She tilted her chin to look at him. 'You mean you've been spying on me?'

'Don't be absurd,' he growled. 'You are a member of my party and therefore warrant my protection.'

'Isn't that—?'

But his kiss suppressed the rest of her words, though he wasn't particularly seeking to silence her—he was simply overcome by a need to connect with her again, and as quickly as possible. He wanted her. Very badly. And judging from the hunger of her own kiss, she was feeling exactly the same way. Her fingers were rubbing frantically through his hair. He could feel the stony jut of her nipples which crowned the soft globes of her breasts. The frenetic beat of his heart, as she pressed against him. All that soft, sweet flesh beneath the deliberately casual clothes she had chosen—yet didn't that subliminal message of independence make him want her even more?

And suddenly Corso wanted to behave wildly—to shrug off the weight of all the duties which had consumed him these past years. To forget the control and restraint and frustration he had imposed upon himself. To smash through the veneer of politeness which governed every move he made. He didn't *want* to be civilised, and take her to the giant arena of his bed. He wanted recklessness and excitement. He wanted to do it to her here. Now. On the floor. And if the truth were known, he wasn't sure if he could make it as far as the bed in his current state of arousal.

It feels this imperative because I'm making up for lost time, he told himself as he tumbled them down onto the Persian rug. But his hand was unsteady as he eased down the zip of her jeans and slid them off to reveal a pair of plain black panties, which were strangely sexy. Moving over the satin of her thighs, he traced his finger over the moist gusset and she quivered as he delved beneath the sensible underwear to find her hot bud.

'Corso!' she gasped as he began to strum her aroused flesh.

'Corso, what?' he demanded silkily, but her eyes had closed and he didn't think she'd even heard him. He liked the fact that her thighs had parted and she was looking as helpless as he felt. He bent his head to her lips, his mouth devouring hers with a hunger which felt elemental as he continued to move his hand against her. Within seconds she was orgasming—moaning his name and writhing beneath him. The scent of her sex was heavy in the air as, with his free hand, he slid down his own zip. He reached for the protection which had been discreetly delivered to his suite earlier, but his fingers were shaking like a drunk's as he lay back on the silken carpet.

And suddenly Rosie was on her knees beside him, smoothing the condom over his erect shaft, and he felt as if he might shatter before he was even inside her. He pulled her on top, so that she was straddling him, and he groaned as she began to ride him. Her eyes were open and they met his gaze unflinchingly and for once he didn't want to look away.

He couldn't look away.

It had never felt like this before. As if the very act of having sex was the lifeblood on which he depended. As if his body needed to feel the heat of hers from the inside. He wanted to know every inch of her. Was it possible to want something at the same time as resenting its power over you? he wondered fleetingly as he she tipped her head back and began to moan, and that was when he let go completely.

When he had recovered his strength, he assumed the dominant position, but even that was not enough to satisfy his carnal hunger as he orgasmed for a second time. The third time left him dazed and utterly replete—and it was only when they were sitting at opposite ends of a steaming bathtub that Corso gave voice to his thoughts.

'I wasn't expecting this,' he said.

She tucked a wet strand of hair behind her ear. 'You mean…the sex?'

'Yes, Rosie,' he replied gravely. The bald word seemed hopelessly inadequate for what had just taken place between them, but he refused to give her false hope by correcting her. 'The sex.'

There was a pause before she answered, a shy smile curving her lips. 'Nor me.'

Life could throw all kinds of things at you, he thought as she lapsed into a contented silence, but it was how you dealt with them which ultimately determined your success, or failure. So much hinged on his forthcoming trip to New York. Things he'd been pushing to the back of his mind, but which had come to haunt him during the hours before dawn, when he'd woken with his heart pounding, his brow wet with sweat, his quest to find his half-brother hazy and nebulous. He still hadn't decided whether or not to initiate a meeting, because to do so could set off a ticking time-bomb. Uncovering the dark secret at the heart of his parents' marriage had taken a lot of discreet detective work but Corso had refused to share his discoveries with anyone else—even the aide who had been with him for longer than he could remember. The fact that it was his secret—and his alone—had allowed him to shrug off the nagging fear that the press might get hold of it. How could they? Nobody could talk to them, because nobody knew.

And the press could always be distracted, couldn't they?

The idea flew into his mind with the blinding certainty of a brainwave and he found himself thinking that the timing of this unforeseen affair could ultimately help his cause. Could his brief relationship with Rosie Forrester provide a smokescreen for the task which lay ahead— and throw any potentially curious journalists off the scent?

And what if that hurts her? nagged the voice of his conscience.

How could it? She'd known from the start that this was only ever going to be temporary. He'd told her so himself, even citing the type of woman he would one day marry. Wouldn't she be honoured if he legitimised their relationship by refusing to hide it away? She might not have any long-term future with him, but she would never be able to say that he had been ashamed of her.

He stared across the steam at the vision she made, with her elbows resting on the sides of the bathtub. Her thick hair was piled high on top of her head, damp tendrils spilling down against her damp cheeks. Although her nipples peeped rosily above the water line, he thought how wholesome she managed to look, and how innocent. Even now. Every time he looked at her, he wanted to be inside her. It was a powerful and visceral instinct. It was unfathomable. And surely, the more he indulged it, the sooner it would go away. *He needed it to go away.* His throat thickened.

'When we go to New York—'

'It's okay, Corso,' she put in quickly. 'I know what you're going to say.'

'Really?' He raised his brows. 'Am I so predictable?'

'You don't have to worry.' She cleared her throat. 'I'm not expecting this to continue when we take the collection to America.'

Beneath the water, he began to massage her ankle. 'Why not?'

'Because…oh! Stop deliberately misunderstanding me!' With a return of customary fire, she slapped her hand on the surface of the water so that bubbles flew above them in disintegrating perfumed clouds. 'You know perfectly well why not! You're a king and I'm your employee.'

'How does that impact on how we spend our downtime?'

'Is that a serious question?'

'Of course it is. There's no need to stop what we're doing—as long as we're both enjoying it.' He slanted her a hooded look. 'And can accept the natural boundaries of such a liaison.'

'You mean we would have to be discreet?' She licked her lips. 'Never be seen in public— that kind of thing?'

He shook his head. 'That's not what I meant, no. We're not doing anything wrong, so I think we should just act normally. And since you're going to be sharing my bed, I see no reason why we shouldn't be seen out together from time to time.' There was a pause. 'But you do need to accept that this is never going to end in a wedding.'

Some people might have considered his words brutal, but not Rosie—because didn't his honesty help squash her occasional pangs of longing for what could never be? He was warning her off. He was advising against nurturing unrealistic dreams about him. But his warning was unnecessary. She knew the rules. She knew them better than anyone. Just as she knew there were a million reasons why she ought to call a halt to this right now. *Before you get in too deep. Before you get your heart broken into a million pieces.*

But every single reason was blown out of the water by the man himself, because who in their right mind would willingly walk away from Corso Andrea da Vignola? Even now she could hardly believe he was here. Tiny droplets of water glittered like diamonds in the fiery depths of his hair and his skin was like oiled silk. She could feel one hair-roughened thigh pressing insistently against hers and already she could sense he wanted her again. She was sitting in a bathtub with the King of Monterosso—yet his exalted position in the world seemed irrelevant. Because it was *him* she wanted. Not his power or his privilege, but him. The man, not the King. And wasn't that the most dangerous thing of all?

'Of course I realise that there isn't going to be a wedding. Even if it's very pompous of you to assume that I'd even want one,' she said coolly.

'So you wouldn't?'

'Oh, I never deal in hypotheticals—it's such a waste of time,' she answered airily. 'But if we're seen together in public, it will invite speculation.'

'Speculation about my love life I can deal with,' he said roughly.

The sudden harshness of his words brought their banter to an abrupt end and Rosie wondered what had made the lines around his mouth deepen like that. But that was irrelevant. This wasn't about trying to burrow her way into his heart or his mind. This wasn't about the future, because they didn't have one. She wasn't going to be needy, or demanding. For the first time in her life she was going to have a bit of fun, with a man who just happened to be a king. And if she found herself back in her cottage in a few weeks' time—alone and missing him—well, surely she'd come through enough stuff in her life to be able to deal with the brief inconvenience of a broken heart.

'So are you going to have dinner with me tonight or not, Rosie?'

'I suppose I am,' she said shakily, because he had started tiptoeing his fingertips all the way up her inner thigh and the bubbled water was slopping over the side of the tub as he found his quivering target.

And suddenly she wasn't thinking at all.

CHAPTER ELEVEN

CORSO DA VIGNOLA WAS AN international superstar.

At least, that was what the New York media were saying—a media desperate for a good news story after a year when the international headlines had been increasingly grim. It seemed that the slick and very cosmopolitan American city couldn't get enough of the striking Mediterranean king and his blonde assistant, who knew so much about his tragic ancestor and her exquisite collection of jewels.

This time, the TV interview which preceded the opening of the collection was shown on one of the country's biggest networks, to a much wider audience than in France. Rosie had to get up at the crack of dawn to appear on a breakfast show featuring an impossibly glamorous presenter with the most perfectly arranged hair she'd ever seen, who seemed much more interested in finding out what the King was *really like*, rather than the provenance of the ancient burial jewels.

'Oh, you know,' Rosie answered, her expression polite but non-committal. 'Like most kings, I suppose.'

'I wouldn't know, as I've never met one. So if he's planning on throwing a big party while he's here...' The presenter's smile was as bright as her hair as her voice tailed off suggestively.

But all publicity was good publicity. At least, that was what they said. As the red light flashed, indicating they were live on air, Rosie sucked in a huge breath and prepared to speak. And this time there were no nerves. All she had to do was to think about the way she seemed to thrill Corso whenever they were alone together. Who wouldn't have acquired a new-found confidence when a man like that kept breathing into her ear how much he wanted her and then showing her exactly how much?

Like all the other embassies, the Monterossian delegation was in Washington and, since Corso had no desire to stay in a hotel, he'd borrowed a Manhattan penthouse from a friend. It was situated a short distance from

Madison Square Park and the quirky museum where the jewels were being showcased. This time the museum's curator was called Donna Green and Rosie found her and her team helpful, welcoming and easy to work with. The downtown location of the apartment meant it was easy for Corso to access the corporate heads he was meeting throughout the day. But first, he insisted that Rosie approve their temporary accommodation, and she couldn't deny being flattered that her opinion mattered to him.

A glass elevator sped them up thirty levels to the very top of an apartment which was like nothing she'd ever seen. Well, of course she hadn't. Even Corso seemed momentarily impressed, and luxury was stamped into his DNA. Spread over five floors and looking as if it were photo-ready for an interiors magazine shoot, the apartment had eleven bedrooms and *fourteen bathrooms* and Rosie found herself worrying aloud that, if she wasn't careful, she might get lost.

'But you do like it?' questioned Corso, turning back from a wall of windows, which showcased the dazzling skyline of the city and the river which gleamed in the afternoon sunshine.

She walked around in a daze, noting the giant glass dining table and carefully placed bowls of pink flowers, which reminded her of the Judas trees she'd seen in Paris. 'Of course I do,' she said. 'Though it's all so perfect it feels a bit like being on a stage set.'

His eyes narrowed thoughtfully. 'Is that how you thought about my palace?'

She thought how few people could say 'my palace' in that proprietorial tone and get away with it. 'Not really. As a child, everything you know is defined by your own experience and it was all I knew. And our house wasn't actually *in* the palace, was it? But, yeah, I guess that since I grew up seeing servants everywhere and watching my parents go off to the occasional formal banquet—I was never particularly daunted by all the splendour.'

'Did you miss it?' he questioned suddenly. 'After you left?'

When he came out with something like that it took Rosie off guard, because it happened so rarely. Corso's preference was always to stay away from the personal and she liked that, because personal questions ran the risk of blurring reality and making her think he cared. Which he didn't. He wasn't laying down the foundations of a long-term relationship by discovering what made her tick. She was his stop-gap lover, that was all. *And if he hadn't been deprived of sex for so long, she wouldn't have got a look-in.*

Sometimes she was afraid that his sizzling gaze would burn right through her, revealing more of herself than she wanted him to see. Scared he might sense that her feelings for him were changing—growing—even if she was doing everything in her power to hold them in check. But surely she should answer him honestly—especially when he had been so honest with her.

'I missed the country,' she said suddenly. 'The beaches and the mountains. And the people, of course. Because nobody makes you feel more welcome than a Monterossian.'

'That's quite some praise, Rosie,' he said softly. 'And on behalf of my people, I thank you.'

The approbation in his voice made her uncomfortable and she couldn't work out why. Because it made her long for more—and then more still? Or because praise made people feel secure and her position with him was anything but secure? 'You're welcome,' she said, determined to maintain a bright façade.

'Let me show you where we'll be sleeping.'

His golden eyes glinted. 'I'm reliably informed that the master bedroom has a monster-sized bed.'

But Rosie wasn't interested in the size of the bed, or yet another breathtaking view over the Hudson River. The only thing which commanded her attention was the man who had dropped to his knees in front of her and begun to remove one of the skyscraper heels she was wearing—at his request.

First one, then the other shoe was thrust away across the silken rug, before he lifted her foot to his mouth and whispered his lips over each bare toe. She gasped aloud as he licked them, slowly. She'd never dreamed that having your toes sucked could be so…erotic. As if hearing her unspoken plea, he pulled her down onto the floor and the journey of his kiss became more focussed. He took his time as his mouth moved slowly up the length of one leg before finding her thighs and Rosie thought she was about to lose her mind. And then he was sliding down her panties and pushing them away, before placing his mouth where she most needed him and beginning to lick his tongue over her.

He teased her until she moaned. Screamed. Squirmed. Holding her hips as if to anchor her, he pressed his mouth harder against her as she began pulsing helplessly, increasing the intensity of her pleasure until at last she lay there, breathless and shaking, her heart thundering with disbelief at the way he could make her feel like this. Every. Single. Time. And each time he did it, she felt a little bit more exposed. As if he were peeling away all the different layers behind which she hid, leaving her raw and susceptible. Could he tell that her emotions were being compromised? Was it a sign of weakness or dependence that made her heart want to burst with joy whenever she looked at him? And both those things were dangerous. So concentrate on the physical, she told herself fiercely—and stop longing for things which are never going to happen.

She opened her eyes to find him watching her and, lazily, drifted her fingers to the hard ridge at his groin.

'Teach me what you like best,' she said, tugging at the belt of his trousers, but he shook his head as she freed him.

'You don't need any teaching, Rosie. You're a—' she saw him swallow as her fingers curled around his erection '—*natural*. You seem to know what I want better than I do myself.'

When she didn't respond, he frowned. 'That was a compliment,' he observed. 'And since

I don't dish them out very often, I find your lack of appreciation a little…disappointing.'

She focussed on his egotism rather than on words which threatened to destabilise her because they were making her feel special and different. And she wasn't. She *wasn't*. 'Would you like me to gush my thanks?' she whispered. 'Or perhaps to demonstrate my gratitude in…other ways.' She bent her head, glad for the concealment of the thick fall of her hair as she took him into her mouth.

She enjoyed his helpless moan as she sucked him—then licked him like a lollipop, trickling the tip of her tongue up and down his hard shaft. She teased him until he was demanding release and, after he had spilled his seed into her mouth, he dug his fingers into her hair and pulled her up to lie on top of him.

'That was…good,' he said unevenly and then, after a moment of silence while he recovered his breath, his next words took her completely by surprise. 'Since there's so much space to choose from, I thought we could have the top two floors of this place to ourselves while we're here.'

Her eyes widened. 'No servants?'

'No servants,' he agreed. 'My staff can easily accommodate themselves in the rest of the apartment. It might be...*interesting* not to have anyone else around. Liberating, don't you think?'

'Very,' she said shakily as he began to unbutton her little cashmere cardigan.

It was early evening by the time they roused themselves, waking up to find themselves tangled together in a bed whose size really had lived up to the hype. Corso yawned. 'Shall I ring down and ask one of my aides to get us a dinner reservation?'

She hesitated. 'Or we could have a meal delivered here. They do great take-out in New York, apparently.'

'Is that what you'd like?'

She nodded. 'We could even ask the aides to organise some shopping so we can make our own breakfast in the mornings.' She rolled onto her stomach, propping herself onto her elbows. 'It means I don't have to dress up and get stared at. It's not very relaxing if all the time you know people are wondering why the King of Monterosso is eating out with someone like me.'

'You don't know what people are thinking, Rosie.'

'*Corso,*' she said patiently. 'Come on. It's always been that way for you. Every move you make and word you speak is analysed.'

He stared out at the lights of the distant skyscrapers and then reached for her. 'True.'

'So let's stay in.'

Corso nodded. 'Let's stay in,' he echoed, the weight of her breast in his hand driving everything else from his mind.

He was aware that she had won that minor battle in the most subtle of ways but unusually he wasn't unduly perturbed at having made a rare concession. Because, in a way, playing house with her distracted him from the fact that somewhere in this city, his brother was walking around. The unwelcome knowledge hovered like a storm cloud on the horizons of his mind. It twisted darkly at his heart. It reminded him that he was here on a mission he had no real appetite for.

Who could blame him for seeking temporary refuge from reality, by losing himself in Rosie's sweet embrace? He'd never thought of sex as a refuge and a comfort before. That it could be layered with things other than satisfaction. And if, from time to time, the sombre toll of his conscience rang too loudly in his ears, it was all too easy to silence it by listening to the more pressing demands of his body.

On the morning of their penultimate day he walked into the kitchen, feasting his eyes on the voluptuous curve of her bottom as she leaned over to poke at something sizzling in a frying pan. Funny. He'd never realised just how sexy an apron could be.

She switched the hob off and turned round, a frown on her face.

'What's wrong?' he questioned as he reached for the coffee pot, even though several weeks ago it wouldn't have occurred to him to enquire after someone's welfare. Or, indeed, to pour them a cup of coffee.

'I'm a bit nervous about going to this cocktail party later,' she said, as he pushed the cup towards her.

Corso tensed. You and me both he thought grimly, though he would never admit to the weakness of nerves. Instead, he threw her a reflective look. 'Why?'

She wiped her hands down the front of her apron. 'I'm not sure if it's a good idea. It's you they want to see, not me. Why, I might even be cramping your style. Didn't you say that representatives from the royal kingdoms of Maraban and Mardivino are going to be attending?' She gave a smile, which looked distinctly forced. 'You never know—your future spouse might be there.'

'I doubt it,' Corso offered drily, lifting the cup to his lips. Didn't she realise he had eyes for no other woman but her? No, of course she didn't. He'd made certain of that. She was inexperienced enough to mistake sexual compatibility for something deeper, and he had been careful not to give her any false hope. Emotional indifference had been a skill he had refined into a veritable art form over the years, and never had he needed it more than he did tonight.

He could feel adrenaline pumping through his body as it prepared for what lay ahead. His heart was racing, his mouth dry. Because tonight was the night. The seemingly innocuous social event he'd planned with the dedicated focus of a military campaign, which would at last bring him into contact with the mysterious billionaire he had no real desire to meet. Whose very existence made a mockery of all that he had believed and been taught to believe.

Xanthos Antoniou.

The man whose blood he shared.

'Corso?'

Rosie's puzzled voice broke into his thoughts. 'Why are you frowning like that?'

He shook his head as if rousing himself from a dream. Or a nightmare. As he walked across the kitchen towards her and pulled her into his arms, he felt the beat of apprehension. And, yes, of fear. What would tonight's reception reveal, and would he live to regret his curiosity?

'I want you by my side tonight,' he instructed harshly, before crushing her mouth with a kiss which left them both breathless.

It all got out of hand, very quickly. Summarily, he dealt with their clothing—removing only the most essential items before bending her over the kitchen table and thrusting into her, to the accompaniment of her mewled cries of pleasure. He blamed his own particularly explosive orgasm for his wandering attention during the rest of day, though he disguised it well enough during back-to-back meetings with CEOs, environmentalists and movers and shakers. But he was glad to get back to the penthouse, and to stand beneath the punishing jets of an icy shower, telling himself that at least the wait was over.

He was staring out at the New York skyline when Rosie emerged from the bedroom wear-

ing a floaty dress the colour of claret, shot
through with threads of silver which echoed
the colour of her eyes. But for once he didn't
compliment her, or allow his eyes to linger on
the bright fall of blonde hair. His head was too
full of conflicting thoughts to offer anything
other than the kind of nod he might give to
one of his drivers.

'Come on,' he said abruptly. 'We need to go.'

Rosie nodded, bewildered by Corso's sudden coolness and change of attitude towards
her and wondering what had caused it, especially as he had been so spontaneous and passionate before he'd left that morning. Was he
already winding down the affair and giving
her a hint of what lay ahead? Because they
were travelling to London the day after tomorrow and once that part of the tour was over...

She shivered as they took the elevator to the
underground car park. After that, she would
probably never see him again. There would
be no reason to. Their very temporary relationship would seamlessly come to an end.
They would say goodbye and Corso would
jet back to Monterosso, preparing for a life
very different from her own. And while he
was selecting the woman who would become
his queen, she and Bianca would be busy buy-

ing Mum a lovely new home. Once that was done she would look round for a job in the art world—for how could she fail to find a decent appointment, with Corso da Vignola as her referee? She ought to be counting her blessings instead of focussing on the dull ache in her heart, which seemed to be growing by the minute. Did she really want to ruin their last few days together by longing for something which could never be hers?

But despite all her attempts at conversation, Corso remained silent and remote during the short car-ride to the exclusive venue and once again she got the sense that he was excluding her. They arrived at the exclusive venue and were shown into an elegant room whose silk-lined walls were studded with old masters. A warm burst of applause greeted Corso's entry and the glittering throng began to converge on her consort.

Rosie listened while he spoke to a couple of prominent politicians, as well as a Hollywood star she recognised—though she'd never seen any of his films—and was ridiculously pleased when a woman came up and told her how much she'd enjoyed going round the exhibition earlier that day.

'The Queen's wedding coronet was just… charming!' she enthused.

Rosie beamed. 'Wasn't it just? All those pearls!'

Dutifully, she ate some sushi and tried to enjoy the beautiful artwork in the room. At one point, she commented on a stunning painting, but Corso didn't appear to have heard her. He had grown completely still and was staring at the door with an expression on his face she'd never seen there before. Following his gaze, she noticed a man who'd just walked in—breaking the cardinal rule that nobody should ever arrive after the royal party.

Rosie blinked, trying to make sense of what was happening. It was weird, because the powerful-looking stranger seemed oddly familiar—even though she was certain she'd never seen him before. He reminded her a bit of Corso, though his hair was black rather than lit with flames and his eyes were black too, not golden. But it wasn't just about his looks. It was the way he held himself—as if he owned the space around him. A woman at his side was gazing up at him with open adoration but he barely seemed to notice her—nor the others of her sex who had turned to study him with predatory interest. Instead, his eyes scanned the room, before coming to rest briefly on Corso. But there was nothing unusual about that because everyone always looked at Corso.

Did she imagine the King's quiet intake of breath or the sudden rigidity of his body as the gazes of the two men clashed? For a moment she thought he was about to walk across the room and greet the stranger—though whether to shake his hand or punch him, she couldn't quite decide—such was the tension radiating from his powerful frame. But instead, he shook his head, as if rousing himself from a deep sleep. Suddenly, he touched his hand to her elbow and let it remain there, the tips of his fingers curving lightly around the crook. It was the most innocent of touches but it was remarkable because it was so unprecedented. And significant. Rosie knew that royals were rarely intimate in public and certainly not with a commoner like her—because such a gesture spoke volumes. She heard a faint murmur as people picked up on it and was aware of heads turning in their direction.

And despite her professed dislike of having people look at her, Rosie felt the warm wash of pleasure sliding over her skin as she started to dream. Who could blame her when he was touching her so proprietorially? She started wondering if maybe this *thing* between them couldn't continue for a while longer and that maybe they could be flexible—or creative— about the future. She didn't want a wedding ring. She wasn't that dumb. She didn't imagine for a moment there could be any kind of permanence in their arrangement—but was it so wrong to want to be with him for as long as possible? If Corso suggested carrying on with the relationship once the tour was over, wouldn't she be crazy not to agree? He had planes, didn't he? And boats. And cars. Travelling between Monterosso and England shouldn't throw up too much of a logistical nightmare. *Why should she give him up if she didn't have to?*

But what if your feelings for him keep growing? taunted a tiny voice inside her head. Aren't you already more than halfway in love with him?

'Come on,' he said, his abrupt tone roughly shattering her reverie. 'We're going.'

'But we've—'

'Don't let me spoil your fun, Rosie. Stay if you want. I can easily arrange for a driver to wait,' he added coolly, dropping his hand from her elbow. 'But I'm leaving.'

It was a terse and inexplicable way to end

the evening and Rosie didn't understand. In the space of a few seconds he had elevated and then trampled on her dreams—and the easy atmosphere between them had suddenly evaporated.

'Is something wrong?' she ventured during the journey back to the apartment.

Was something wrong?

Corso wondered what she would say if he told her the truth—that suddenly all his certainties about life had been smashed. He clenched one fist to mimic the hard clench of his heart. He had always thought of himself as unique. The sole heir, born to rule. That had been a given—the one constant, which impacted on everything and everyone around him. Even in his most contemplative moments, he had rationalised that seeing his illegitimate half-brother for the first time would have no real effect on him.

But he had been wrong.

Laying eyes on Xanthos in the flesh had felt visceral. Powerful. Unsettling. A sombre connection to the past, and… He swallowed. Because only a fool would ignore the possibility of how it might impact on his future.

'Corso?' prompted Rosie's voice at his elbow and he looked down at her upturned face, to see concern written in her grey eyes. And, oh, the temptation to confide in her was overwhelming—because didn't he trust her gentle common sense and honesty? Wouldn't her uncomplicated softness be like a soothing balm, taking some of the sting out of his discovery?

But he would not do that. It was not fair. Not to him and especially not to her. She was a temporary fixture who would soon be gone— so why on earth would he tell her?

'Nothing's wrong,' he bit out, turning away from the brief hurt which clouded her expression.

He excused himself when they returned to the penthouse, citing urgent work which required his attention. He was still at his desk at midnight, when she hovered in the doorway, her blonde hair lit from the light in the hallway behind her. She was wearing a silky night-gown the colour of ice, edged with a darker lace which emphasised the creamy swell of her breasts. But if she was hoping to seduce him, he was going to disappoint her. He wanted to be alone with his thoughts, not to answer any of the questions he could see were still written in her eyes.

'You go to bed without me,' he said, and he

saw the disappointment which made her bite her lip before nodding and turning away.

It was only after she had gone that he realised this was the first time they hadn't gone to bed together.

CHAPTER TWELVE

Rosie woke just as dawn was filtering through the windows, opening her eyes to discover Corso hadn't bothered to activate the electric blinds which usually blotted out the New York morning. He lay beside her, his eyes closed. Dark lashes feathered the autocratic cheekbones and the pale sunlight emphasised the fiery highlights of his dark hair. She thought about snuggling up to him as she usually would have done. Wrapping her arms around his warm body and trailing soft kisses up his neck and reaching down to curl her fingers around his inevitable erection. But something was holding her back. A niggle in the back of her mind, which was refusing to be silenced.

And that was when it hit her.

She thought about Corso's behaviour last night. His tension at the party when the stranger had walked in and the unmistakable mirroring between the two men. The way he had withdrawn from her in the car on the way home and his chilly distance when they'd arrived back at the penthouse. Who *was* the black-eyed incomer who had arrived after the royal party last night? She sucked in a breath and Corso's eyes opened so quickly that she wondered if he'd been awake all along.

'That man,' she said.

The hardening of his mouth became an ugly slash. 'Which man?'

Her heart began to pound, because didn't that sound awfully like evasion? 'The man at the party. The man who arrived after you. With the black hair.'

'What about him?'

But he pushed aside the sheet and got out of bed without touching her and that had never happened before. Rosie blinked. His face was forbidding. His expression icy. And this was a Corso she had forgotten existed—or had conveniently allowed herself to forget. The emotionally distant monarch who ruled everyone around him. Who subtly controlled the comments of others by default—even if he had no power over their thoughts. She felt confused—and vulnerable. But she needed to hold it together. She mustn't jump to conclusions, because perhaps Corso needed her help. He certainly looked as if he needed *something*—for the emptiness in his eyes was making him look so bleak and lost and troubled.

'You know him,' she said.

'I've never met him before in my life.'

She wondered whether she should just shut up, which was obviously what he wanted her to do. But she couldn't just walk away and pretend this wasn't happening. She was in too deep to be able to do that. She wanted to reach out and comfort him—even if she didn't know why he seemed to be in need of comfort. Something was driving her on to find out what this was all about…and what did she have to lose? 'But you know who he is, don't you?'

The silence was so long that Rosie wondered whether he hadn't heard her, or was just choosing to ignore her question.

'Yes, I do,' he ground out and she saw the lines on his face becoming deep crevices, before he turned away to haul on a pair of jeans and tug a T-shirt over his ripped torso. And when he turned back his eyes were no longer bleak, they were blazing with a pure, bright gold—as if he were about to go into battle. 'His name is Xanthos Antoniou,' he grated. 'And he is my father's son.'

She stared at him in confusion, trying to make sense of his words. 'Your father's son?' she repeated and immediately thought about all the possible repercussions. 'Is he—?'

'Older,' he bit out, as if correctly anticipating her question.

'I don't understand,' she said. 'Why is this the first we've ever heard of him?'

Corso registered her bewilderment and suddenly he wanted to lash out. Wanted to deflect some of his pain and confusion onto someone else. Someone who wasn't him. *We?* he echoed imperiously. 'Why would you be privy to such knowledge, Rosie?'

'I'm sorry.' She flushed. 'That was presumptuous of me.'

But to Corso's anger, his icy reaction was not enough to deter her, because she sat up in bed a little, her grey eyes huge in her pinched face.

'Tell me,' she urged softly. 'Tell me what this is all about, Corso.'

He stared at her and felt the tightening of his throat. She looked so soft. So giving. As if she wanted to open up her arms to him and hold him tight. He wanted to tell her to keep her questions to herself and stop being so damned supportive—because he didn't need her support. He didn't need anything or anyone—

yet he felt as if he might explode if the words stayed locked inside him much longer.

He drew in a ragged breath before baldly presenting the facts—as if that would minimise their impact. 'It took me a long time to go through my father's papers,' he began slowly. 'And it was only when I was nearing the end that I discovered a letter which had been hidden away. It had been written many years ago.' He paused. 'Thirty-four years, to be exact.'

She nodded, pulling up the duvet so it reached her chin.

'It was a letter from a woman, saying she had just given birth to my father's child.' He turned away because he didn't want to see what was written in Rosie's eyes. Not pity, nor pain, nor empathy. 'And attached to the letter was a note in my mother's handwriting, which ended with the words—*are we ever going to talk about this, Joaquin?*'

'Do you think they ever did?' she questioned at last, into the vast silence which followed.

He shrugged, but his shoulders were heavy. 'Who knows? From the date of the note, my mother must have been very sick because she died soon after that.' His words felt painful. Like stones lodged in the dryness of his throat. 'Nobody knows about it—not even Rodrigo,' he added harshly as he turned again to look at her. 'Only the detective who tracked Xanthos down. And now you.'

'And does he—Xanthos—realise who he really is?'

'I have no idea.'

She pleated her brow, like someone trying to work out the final clue of a crossword puzzle. 'So what were you—are you—planning to do with this information? Surely it wasn't enough to catch a glimpse of him at a party and then just leave?'

'I hadn't thought it through. I still haven't. It was a greater shock than I had anticipated,' he admitted roughly. 'Seeing him in the flesh like that.'

'Yes. I can imagine it was. But…' She hesitated. 'You can't just let this opportunity go, Corso. You just can't. You've dared to dig the secret out and examine it and that's a really brave thing to do.'

She smiled at him and it was the sweetest smile he'd ever seen. So why had his heart started aching, as if something very sad and inevitable were about to happen? As if he had anticipated what her next words were going to be…

'I mean, it's such an incredible coincidence

that he happened to be in the same city at all, isn't it?' And when he didn't answer she searched his face and he saw the beginnings of a frown begin to appear. It happened almost in slow motion. He watched as she stared down at the sheet, as if searching for spots of coffee they might have spilled there, and when she looked up again her mouth was twisted, as if she'd just touched her tongue to her teeth and tasted something very bitter. 'But it wasn't like that, was it, Corso?' she said slowly. 'Bringing the collection to New York and managing to see your half-brother at the same time wasn't just a huge coincidence.'

'Does it matter?'

'Actually, I think it does.' She sat up straight, pushing her untidy hair away from cheeks which were suddenly very flushed. 'The whole tour was planned in order to make that happen, wasn't it?'

There was a moment of complete and breathless quiet.

'What if it was?' he demanded harshly. 'What difference does it make?'

Rosie heard the irritation in his voice and the dismissal, too. Yes, there was definitely dismissal—along with that innate sense of entitlement which was never far from the surface. His royal authority superseded everything and woe betide anyone who allowed themselves to forget that. He might have tolerated her feistiness before—but that had been as lovers, when it was all a bit of a game. And this was no longer a game. He would no longer tolerate her insurrection or advice, because this was too important. This had been his main objective all along and everything else had been an irrelevance.

Including her.

'That's why you didn't mind being seen with me, isn't it?' she said slowly, her gaze not leaving his. 'Why you wanted to eat out when we arrived here. Because you know it would encourage the press to take our photos and wonder about the exact nature of our relationship. It would prevent the media from fishing around and finding out the real reason why you might be in New York, wouldn't it? I suppose I must have put a spanner in the works by telling you I'd prefer to eat in and not make a fuss.' She gave a bitter laugh. 'What a disappointment I must have been, Corso—when any other woman would have moved heaven and earth to be seen with you in public. That's why you touched me at the reception last night, wasn't it? Knowing people would notice and it would send their imaginations into overdrive. It would override the fact that you'd been staring across the room at a stranger who looked like you, and stop anyone from asking why. You're not going to deny that, are you, Corso? At least do me the courtesy of telling the truth.'

She saw a muscle working at his temple but that was the only thing about him which moved, because the tension was making his body look as if it had been carved from rock. How he must loathe this kind of analysis, she thought—trying to convince herself she felt no pity for him as he nodded, his expression grim.

'Yes, you're right. I plead guilty to all your accusations. I saw an opportunity and I took it.' His voice harshened. 'But while I might have decided to capitalise on our relationship once we'd become lovers, I didn't actively set out to seduce you. That was never part of my plan. I didn't have sex with you in order to use you. You must believe that, Rosie.'

No, he had seduced her because he had gone without sex for seven long years, and she had been available—falling into his arms like a ripe piece of fruit dripping from the tree. In a way it might have been a lot more flattering if he *had* intended to seduce her.

And he *had* used her, that was the bottom line. He'd used her just as surely as that scammer had used her mother. He'd used her as a smokescreen. A distraction. All the while she'd been thinking how close they'd become and how easy it would be to love him—he had been busy guarding all his secrets.

Rosie stared at the man who stood like a towering colossus against the glorious New York sunrise. In jeans and T-shirt, with the hint of new beard shadowing his jaw, his outward appearance wasn't the least bit regal—yet his extraordinary power radiated from every pore of his body.

She had often wondered how this strange affair of theirs might end. Whether she would be grown-up enough to wish him well for the dynastic marriage he'd spoken of, which featured somewhere in his future. She'd never imagined it would be like this—with a sense of bitter hurt and betrayal seeping through her veins like poison.

Unwilling to rise naked from the bed in front of him, she gave him a tight smile. 'I wonder if you wouldn't mind leaving me alone now, Corso? Because I'd like to pack.'

His eyes narrowed. 'What are you talking about?'

'What do you think I'm talking about? I'm going back to England. So first I'm going to pack and then I'd like Rodrigo to arrange my transport back home.'

His frown deepened. 'But we still have the London leg of the tour to do.'

He meant it. That was the worst part. He didn't stop to consider how *she* might be feeling after his astonishing revelation. 'Did you honestly think we were just going to carry on as before?' she demanded. 'With me meekly helping mount another major exhibition as if nothing has happened and, what—still sharing your bed at night?'

'I don't see why not.' He shrugged with what looked like genuine confusion. 'I don't understand why you're so angry, Rosie.'

He had her on the spot now and she guessed what was making her most angry was the realisation of how little she really meant to him. But her pride would never let her admit to that. 'I wish you'd told me,' she said stubbornly. 'About your brother.'

'Why should I? That would imply an intimacy between us which I have never sought. Not with you. Not with anyone, if you want the truth.' He lifted up the palms of his hands with an air of impatient query. 'Just what did you expect, Rosie?' he breathed. 'It was only ever intended to be a casual affair, we both knew that. I'm returning to Monterosso imminently and they are lining up suitable princesses for me to make my choice of bride.'

'Already?' she burst out, before she could stop herself.

'It's going to be sooner rather than later.' He paused, his next words very deliberate. 'I need an heir.'

She flinched. She couldn't help herself and, although she knew she had said enough, she couldn't seem to hold back the bitter words. 'And will you promise your future bride your fidelity, even if you can't promise her your heart?'

His face became a disdainful mask as he stopped to consider this, as if she had finally overstepped the line. But maybe he decided to answer her question anyway—as if by doing that he would finally kill off any last, lingering hopes. 'Of course I can,' he said coolly. 'Seven years of total celibacy has reassured me that I need never stray.'

She could have hit him, yet in the midst of Rosie's pain came the knowledge that he was capable of so much more. That he didn't *have* to hide behind the emotional barriers he'd erected during a difficult childhood, spent with a dying mother and a distant father. He *could* learn to love—of that she was sure. Hadn't there been moments when she'd seen a chink in his armour, when he had shown her glimpses of the man she knew he could be?

'You've got to open yourself up to love, Corso,' she whispered, aware of the faint prick of tears in the backs of her eyes. 'You've got to learn to love the woman you marry, or else your life will be empty. Just like you've got to get to know your brother, because he's the only brother you're ever going to have.'

Now the disdain was back, and this time it was here to stay. 'I think we've said enough, don't you? I'll speak to Rodrigo about your transportation. Goodbye, Rosie.'

'Just one more thing,' she said as he turned away, and as he faced her again she could see the flicker of apprehension on his features. Did he think she was about to make a total fool of herself? To beg his forgiveness for her presumptuousness and tell him she'd changed her mind and would take him on whatever terms she could get?

'What is it?'

'I just want to be sure that I'm still going to get paid, even if I'm cutting short my involvement in the tour.'

His mouth twisted, as if her words had in

some way reassured him. 'Don't worry, Rosie. You'll still get your money.'

And then he was gone. Tears blurred her eyes but Rosie dashed to the shower and brushed them away with an impatient fist before layering her clothes into her suitcase as fast as she could. The exquisite designer outfits she left hanging there—glittering symbols of a different time. She gave a bitter smile. She would have no need of couture when she was back in her old life.

A chauffeur-driven car was waiting to take her to the airport and somewhere over the Atlantic she was able to get a message to her sister, announcing her arrival time in the UK and wondering if they might be able to meet up next weekend, in order to begin the process of getting their mother settled. She was wondering if—and how much—she was going to tell Bianca. Why rake up something which was probably better left forgotten?

The last thing Rosie expected was to see her sister standing waiting for her at the Arrivals exit, her glossy black hair piled up in a sleek updo, oblivious to the men who were giving her second and sometimes third glances.

'What are you doing here?' whispered Rosie as the two women hugged tightly.

'I thought I'd surprise you as that text from the plane didn't sound like you at all. You look… *Rosie!* What on earth is the matter? You look *terrible!*'

Rosie didn't trust herself to reply, but by the time they'd reached Bianca's car she had started crying and the two of them sat in the airport car park, while outside rain lashed down wildly from a gunmetal sky. She'd held herself in check throughout the flight but now she was home and reality had started sinking in, she couldn't seem to hold back the tears any longer and they streamed down her cheeks.

'You've been having a relationship with Corso?' Bianca verified in amazement, when Rosie's choked words had become comprehensible.

'Yes! It's okay. Call me a fool and I would agree with you—because he's a…brute! A cold-hearted and unfeeling brute and I hate him. *Hate* him!' She waited for guaranteed words of support because Bianca had never been Corso's biggest fan, but to Rosie's surprise, no such words came.

'You do realise,' ventured Bianca cautiously, 'that he sent me a massive cheque to buy Mum a house, a couple of weeks ago?'

Rosie blinked, as if her sister had suddenly started speaking in a foreign language. 'But I hadn't done any work for him then,' she said in confusion. And she certainly hadn't been sleeping with him at that point. 'Why didn't you tell me?'

'He asked me not to. He was very insistent you shouldn't know.'

'What...what did he say?'

'That we should get Mum out of London as quickly as possible, so she could be close to her sister. Only we should put the house in our joint names, in case she was tempted to give all her money away again to some chancer she might meet on the Internet. In fact, I've got a few places lined up. I thought we could go and look at them with her, this weekend. Wasn't that kind of him?'

'Wasn't it?' said Rosie weakly.

'It made me think that maybe I'd misjudged him in the past. Now I'm not so sure.'

Rosie nodded and fumbled in her bag for a tissue. But in a way, it made everything even harder to bear. She didn't want to think of Corso as being considerate, and looking out for her mother. She wanted to think of him as the man who had...

What?

Given her the most blissful time of her life but neglected to tell her something which was deeply personal to him? Wasn't she behaving like a child who looked into a toy-shop window and demanded *all* of the toys?

She tried to put on a cheerful front—not just for her own sake, but for others too. She didn't want Bianca to worry about her, and made her promise not to breathe a word to their mother. And even though she felt empty and distracted, she managed to celebrate getting her degree and resolved to start looking round for a job in the art world, once she felt a bit more like herself.

But then the articles started appearing in the sort of colourful magazines you found at supermarket checkouts and Rosie found herself buying them and slavishly reading them, despite knowing it was only piling on the agony. Articles about Corso and his hunt for a royal wife. All with the same stomach-churning theme along the lines of: *Who Will Wear the Monterossian Glass Slipper?*

There were accompanying photographs, too—and that made it even worse because Rosie started comparing herself unfavourably to the sleek beauties who seemed practically perfect in every way. Her eyes scanned every image with forensic intensity as she searched Corso's ruggedly handsome features for clues about which one he liked best. For a while it seemed as if the cute redheaded equestrian from Boritavia was a serious contender, until she was replaced by a dark-headed beauty from Mardivino.

Rosie screwed up the magazine and hurled it into the recycling bin, telling herself that she needed to face up to reality.

Corso was going to marry somebody else and, yes, her heart was breaking. But so what? One day she would get over it.

And then the invitations started arriving. Old-fashioned cards written in black ink and delivered in thick, buff-coloured envelopes— inviting her to attend interviews at some of London's most famous art galleries. They all mentioned her work in Paris and New York and said she came highly recommended. And you wouldn't need to be a genius to know who was behind these surprising requests.

Corso.

He was intervening on her behalf, just as he'd provided the money for her mother's new home. Rosie's fingers were shaking as she put down one of the letters and, several days later, she went along to the prestigious Brian Allen Institute, where her interview went much better than she could ever have imagined.

'We'd like to offer you a job,' said the owner of the famous art gallery.

'Honestly?'

His kind and clever face relaxed into a smile. 'Honestly,' he affirmed. 'If you'd like to accept it?'

'Oh, yes, I would,' said Rosie hastily. 'Yes, please.'

Using her concessionary railcard, she took the train back to Reading and worked out what she would say in her resignation letter to her manager, who had always been so kind to her. She would wait until she was properly settled in her new role and then she could send Corso a beautiful postcard, thanking him for everything he had done—diplomatically avoiding the subject of their brief affair, which in retrospect, should have been avoided. She would choose an old master painting on very expensive card and it would bear a carefully constructed message, which was light and witty, without seeming in the least bit bitter, or resentful.

She would have to choose the time of writing very carefully, of course.

It would be a terrible give-away if the words on her carefully chosen postcard were obliterated by tears.

CHAPTER THIRTEEN

THE SOUND OF the storm split the night. Thunder boomed like the clash of cymbals, while silver-white lightning forked the sky. Heavy rain was lashing relentlessly against the windows when Rosie heard a knock at the door and she frowned—because who in their right mind would be out on a night like this?

It must be the wind, she thought. Perhaps a falling branch tumbling onto the house. The forest demonstrating its own elemental power.

But no.

There it was again. Definitely a knock.

She checked the spyhole and thought she must be hallucinating. That perhaps she had conjured up a rainswept image of the man who was always hovering at the edges of her mind. She battled to open the door against the tug of the wind and when she finally managed it, her breath dried in her throat. Because this was no illusion. It was real. Corso da Vignola standing there like some avenging angel, seemingly oblivious to the rain which poured down on him. Wordlessly, she opened the door wider and he stepped inside, his black overcoat and dark hair completely sodden, and Rosie's heart was pounding as she shut the door on the howling night.

A shot of pain ripped through her like a bullet because it was six months since she'd seen him. Six agonisingly slow months during which she'd thrown herself into her new job—while Corso had been busy choosing his new queen. Half a year of living with a constant ache in her heart and wondering why the world around her seemed so grey, even on the brightest of summer days.

Yet now that he was here, it gave her no real pleasure. What pleasure could be gained from reacquainting herself with the devilish gleam of his eyes, or the muscular power of his body and the quiet strength which emanated from it? Didn't acknowledging his golden-dark beauty only drive home just how desperately she missed him?

'You're soaking,' she said woodenly. 'Put your coat by the fire and I'll make some tea.'

'I don't want tea.'

'Well, I do.'

Actually, what she wanted was the opportunity to prepare herself for what she suspected might be the reason why he had turned up like this, without announcement. What was it he wanted to say? To warn her about something she would soon see in the papers—that he was marrying a suitable princess at last?

I thought it only courteous to let you know myself, he would say.

That was very thoughtful of you, she would reply.

She hurried out into the kitchen and returned a few minutes later, thinking how pathetic it was that she'd loaded up the tray with her best china. Unless she really thought the King of Monterosso was going to be impressed by a few cups and saucers she'd picked up in the Debenhams closing down sale, when in his palace they regularly supped from precious, blood-red porcelain.

But Corso didn't appear to have noticed her return—or, if he did, he didn't acknowledge it. His back was to her as he gazed into the fire burning brightly in the grate, and his body was completely motionless. He was still wearing his coat, she registered dully, so clearly he wasn't planning to stay long. She put the tray down with a clatter and as he turned to look at her she felt a moment of despair, tinged with a much healthier edge of anger. *Why* had he come here today—making her endure all the pain of saying goodbye to him all over again?

'What do you want, Corso?' she questioned quietly. 'I assume you weren't just passing?'

Corso studied her across the distance of the small room, which suddenly seemed as vast as one of the ballrooms in his palace. The only sound he could hear was the crackle of the fire and the fierce pounding of his heart and as he met her quizzical stare he wondered what she would say if he admitted the truth. That he was here because he had to be. Because it felt as if something were drawing him here, without his permission—like the flights of wild geese which flew north in summer, compelled by a biological imperative outside their control.

Yet for weeks now, he had been fighting an inner battle with himself, asking if what he was about to do was in Rosie Forrester's best interests. Or just his own. He had decided to choose his words with care. To lay down the foundations for what was to be his core message—just as if he were presenting a business meeting to foreign investors. But his mouth was stubbornly refusing to obey his thoughts.

'No.' He paused, unfamiliar with the language of love and need. And scared of it, too. He who had never been scared of anything. 'I've come to tell you how much I've missed you.'

She shook her head and her loose blonde hair swayed like an armful of corn. 'Please don't tell me things which are patently untrue. I've seen the photos, Corso—and I've read the articles in gruesome and gushing detail. You've been working your way through every eligible royal princess on the planet, we both know that.'

'Because I felt I had to!' he declared. 'It was something I needed to do.'

'There's no need to make it sound like some sort of punishment,' she accused hotly. 'Not when every single one of those women was accomplished and beautiful!'

'Yes, they were,' he conceded.

'How wonderful for you.'

He heard the crack of emotion in her voice and he couldn't bear the thought that he had hurt her. *Was* hurting her. And wasn't there the inconceivable possibility she might not find it in her heart to forgive him?

'In New York I was reeling from so many things,' he said slowly. 'Not least, my relationship with you and the way it was making me feel. It had never been that way with a woman before—that simple or that easy. That blissful, if you must know.'

'Corso—'

'And then I saw my half-brother across the room,' he said, cutting through her whispered protest. 'And suddenly, I wasn't thinking straight. I found myself filled with a primitive desire to secure my legacy—a legacy which had been drummed into me for as long as I remember.'

'To produce an heir?' she said, in a small voice.

'To produce an heir,' he echoed. 'So I went back to Monterosso and did what I considered to be my duty. I was shown princess after princess. There were sheikhas and sultanas. Countesses and duchesses. But none of them...' His voice shook, husky and helpless with intent. 'None of them were you, Rosie. And that's why I can't marry any of them.'

'Corso...please... Don't.'

'Don't what?' he demanded. 'Don't admit you're the only person in the world who tells me the truth? Who is always fighting my corner, even when I don't deserve it. Even when I hurt you—you were still looking out for me. Your jealousy didn't impact on your generosity. You told me that I needed to open up my heart to my future wife, or my life would be empty. But you know something?' He stared at her. 'The only thing which will make my life empty is not having you in it.'

He could see the glimmer of tears which were making her stormy eyes look rain-filled and remembered the quick squeeze of the arm she'd given him, after his mother had died. He wanted to kiss her. To hold her and cradle her against the rapid pounding of his heart. But for too long he had thought about what *he* wanted and this needed to be about her.

'Corso,' she said, but he shook his head.

'Let me finish, Rosie. Please. Because you need to hear this. All of it.' He stared down at the blue Monterossian vase on the table, which was filled with bright sprigs of autumn berries. 'You told me I'd be crazy not to connect with my brother and deep down I knew you were right, even though I baulked at the thought. My father had been a cold and distant man but until the discovery of the letter, I'd always thought his marriage to my mother was completely faithful. That was the version I was led to believe.' He paused. 'I didn't want to confront the reality that he'd been conducting a love affair with another woman, and giving his other son all the attention he never gave me.' He gave a bitter smile. 'But I pushed aside the residual traces of childhood jealousy and telephoned Xanthos, suggesting we meet up.'

She nodded, her gaze intent. 'What did he say?'

'He agreed—reluctantly. I flew to Berlin, and so did he.'

'And was the meeting…a success?'

Corso heard the breath of hope in her voice. He shook his head. 'Not really. It seems my construct of the whole situation was completely wrong. Xanthos had never even met my— our—father. His mother had been only eighteen when she'd had him and I gather it was…' suddenly it was difficult to hold back his disdain and his judgement '…a transactional, rather than an emotional relationship. He *paid* to have sex with her,' he explained baldly and saw her look of bafflement turn into shock. 'That's all he would tell me,' he concluded grimly. 'And I don't blame him.'

She nodded, her blonde hair shimmering in the firelight. He could practically see her mind working. But unsurprisingly, she didn't fixate on any of the more salacious aspects of the whole affair. Instead she turned her ocean-grey gaze to him. 'Do you think you'll meet again?'

Corso shrugged. 'Who knows? We'll have to wait and see. He had a tough time.'

'You didn't have it so great yourself,' she pointed out. 'Your dad was never around and when he was, he was remote—we all knew that. And then your mum died.'

'That's why I used to hang around at your place,' he said, his next admission coming from somewhere he'd never dared access before. 'Because it felt like home.'

'Oh, Corso.'

But he steeled his heart against the tenderness in her voice because he still wasn't done. 'My last royal date took place three months ago, which might make you wonder why I didn't come and explain all this before. But I wanted you to make the most of your new job and your new life. To have the opportunity to work in your chosen field and decide whether or not you wanted to continue in it.' He paused and suddenly his throat was so dry that he was finding it difficult to breathe. 'Or whether you would be prepared to give it all up and marry me.'

There was the clattering sound of a teaspoon being dropped to the floor. 'What are you saying?' she demanded suspiciously, as if he were having a joke at her expense.

'I want to marry you, Rosie Forrester. Because I love you and the thought of not being with you is unendurable. I need to know if you can ever forgive me for my lack of insight. For my arrogance and stupidity. For the way I rode roughshod over your feelings and didn't take them into account. I need you to know that I'm sorry, truly sorry. But most of all, I need to know if you'll be my wife.'

'But we…can't, Corso. You know we can't.'

'Why not?'

'Because Monterosso wants you to marry a royal princess.'

'Monterosso wants their king to be happy and you are the key to my happiness.' He let out a ragged sigh. 'I'd convinced myself I didn't feel the things which other men claim to feel—that I was immune to love and to emotion—but I was wrong. Because you brought something to life in me, Rosie Forrester. You took my cold and unfeeling heart and opened it up. You made me love you and I need…' He sucked in a deep breath. 'I need to know how you feel about me.'

Her gaze was very bright and very clear. 'You know exactly how I feel about you, Corso,' she whispered.

'Tell me,' he whispered back.

'I love you,' she said simply. 'You. The man. And that's all I want. To live with you and lie with you.' Her voice trembled. 'To be your support by day and your lover at night. To feel your child moving within me—many children, if we're lucky enough to have them. To fill that big palace of yours with love and make it a real home. That's what I want.'

His lips curved. 'Not palaces, nor diamonds, or fancy yachts which skim the ocean?'

She shook her head. 'Those things aren't important.'

'To some people they are.' He brushed a strand of hair away from her cheek. 'Me included, if you must know.'

She frowned. 'I didn't think you were into status symbols.'

'Status symbol or not, you're going to need a very big diamond if you're going to become my wife,' he said drily. 'But you do realise what you're taking on, don't you? Because you know better than anyone the demands of royal life. Constantly being on show. Having every look and word you utter analysed for nuance, or meaning. You're going to have to learn never to give too much of yourself away, Rosie, and

I'm afraid that your trust in people will inevitably become eroded—'

'And you're going to have to learn to stop being so suspicious and start giving people the benefit of the doubt,' she interrupted passionately. 'To realise it's not the end of the world if sometimes you wear your heart on your sleeve—because your people will respect a king who isn't afraid of being in touch with his own feelings, rather than someone buttoned-up and inflexible.'

'Am I buttoned-up and inflexible?' he questioned gravely.

'Sometimes. But I can show you how to change. We can help each other grow, can't we?'

'Is that a yes to my proposal?' he questioned wryly.

'It is,' she agreed, looking suddenly shy as he reached into his pocket and produced a small box before withdrawing a ring of radiant brilliance—the incandescent diamond flashing like an explosion of white fire within the tiny room.

'Oh, Corso,' she said as he got down onto one knee before her.

'You're going to tell me that you've changed your mind about big diamonds after all?'

She shook her head. 'I'm going to tell you

that I love you,' she whispered as he slid the mighty rock onto her finger. 'I love you more than words can ever say.'

EPILOGUE

A LOUD POP woke her, and Rosie blinked open her lashes to focus on the glorious room. The setting sun gilded the sofa on which she lay, naked and replete beneath a soft, cashmere blanket. From here she could see the lake and the mighty mountain which dominated the distant horizon. At the far end of the room stood an enormous fir tree, decked with tiny star-like lights and gleaming silver baubles, for in two days time it would be Christmas.

And there was her husband, his magnificent body bare save for a small white towel slung low on his sexy hips, holding two crystal flutes filled with champagne, which he carried across the room towards her.

'Happy honeymoon,' he said softly.

Rosie smiled a little giddily as he put the glasses down, before dropping the tiny towel to the floor and getting underneath the blanket next to her.

'I can hardly believe we're married,' she admitted, reveling in the warmth of his delicious flesh.

He cupped one breast, stroking his thumb over the nipple. 'Did you enjoy the day?'

'Every moment,' she said, her voice catching a little. Because it had been an emotional experience. A wedding just before Christmas was always going to tug at the heartstrings, even before you factored in the significance of this particular ceremony.

They'd been married in the Monterossian cathedral—a magnificent structure which towered over the city of Esmelagu, and from which you could see the capital's famous lake. Watched by her mother, sister, aunt and some of her co-workers from the railway—Rosie had spoken the solemn vows which had made her Corso's queen.

She had worn a lavishly embroidered white gown—her flowing veil held in place by Queen Aurelia's ancient coronet. There had been tears in her mother's eyes at that point, as she'd whispered how proud Rosie's father would have been.

But despite the rejoicing of the wedding

guests, and of the Monterossian people who had taken Rosie into their hearts—the wedding day hadn't passed without a faint sense of uncertainty and of matters unresolved.

Because Xanthos—the King's half-brother, had been there—looking as if it were the last place on earth he wanted to be. His attendance had been grudging and loaded with conditions, some of which had stretched Corso's patience at the time. Unwilling to publicly acknowledge his fraternal link with the Monterossian King, it seemed the half-Greek billionaire had no desire to trade on his royal connections.

He hadn't seemed to hit it off with Bianca either, which was a bit unfortunate, as Rosie had arranged for Xanthos to fly her sister back to England. Bianca had reacted badly to this piece of news—behaving as if she was being expected to slum it, instead of travelling in total luxury on a private jet.

'Why are you frowning?' questioned Corso, as he turned his attention to her other breast.

'I'm just thinking how difficult siblings can be at times.'

'That much is true,' he said softly. 'I guess we just have to let some things go. At least, that's what you always tell me.'

Corso narrowed his eyes as he tried not to be distracted by the pert thrust of her nipple. What was it she'd said to him when he had wondered aloud why Xanthos seemed so determined to dislike him? 'Everything has its time, my darling. We just have to be patient, and wait.'

He believed her. Just like he believed everything she said, because Rosie was the most honest and decent person he had ever met and it was the first time he had ever truly trusted another person. Sometimes he felt like pinching himself because he'd never believed that life could be this good. This easy. And it was all down to her. To this woman who loved him in a way he'd never thought he could be loved. Who had broken down the barriers with which he had surrounded himself and let the light in.

His people loved her and he loved her and one day soon he wanted her to have his baby.

He turned his head to study her blonde head, which was resting comfortably on his shoulder, and she lifted her gaze to his. 'You haven't touched your champagne,' he observed.

'Neither have you.'

'Because I can think of things I'd much rather do than drink,' he growled as he drifted his fingertips to her peaking breast. 'Like making love to my wife.'

'But we've only just—'

He silenced her half-hearted protest with first one kiss and then another and soon she was straddling him on the gilded sofa and tossing back her mane of magnificent hair.

Outside, the setting sun was turning the mountain into the startling colour which had given the country its name.

And, within the sanctuary of their bedroom, the King and Queen of Monterosso made sweet love.

* * * * *

If you thought
Stolen Nights with the King
was swoon-worthy then you're sure to love
the next instalment in the
Secrets of the Monterosso Throne duet,
coming soon!
In the meantime why not dive into these other
Sharon Kendrick stories?

Cinderella's Christmas Secret
One Night Before the Royal Wedding
Secrets of Cinderella's Awakening
Confessions of His Christmas Housekeeper
Penniless and Pregnant in Paradise

Available now!